Potter's Image

My Personal Relationship With God

Leon Coates

Library of Congress Control Number: 2002117386
ISBN 1-591604-15-X

Xulon Press
10640 Main Street
Suite 204
Fairfax, VA 22030
(703) 934-4411
XulonPress.com

To order additional copies, call 1-866-909-BOOK (2665).

Dedication

I want to give all glory and honor to my Father God Jehovah who so patiently, tenderly, loving and through His wisdom, this book came into being a reality. I stand in amazement of His moves and ways at all times.

Also I give much thanks and gratitude to Beverly Gould, who gave of herself to the Father God Almighty during the many hours of time involved in this book.

All Glory to Father God

Introduction

L et me tell you a little about my past life on this earth; yes, I do very much understand what a lot of you are going through. You see, all my life, I felt out of place, not belonging, not being wanted or accepted, always the feeling of being alone and no one ever seemed to care or wanted to be around me; and yes, to the place of feeling confused and frustrated, sometimes to the point of being weary, rejected, and tired; and you can bet, and believe that the enemy did his part in keeping me in this realm and intensifying it. What I have just mentioned shows us a small portion of what our Messiah Jesus Christ experienced for you and me. The things that I have mentioned that I experienced was on an individual basis—the things that He experienced was taking on everything for you and me and everybody that has been and ever will be on this universe. Do you find words capable of describing all this on Jesus' consuming experiences? He experienced and carried our grief's, our weaknesses, our sicknesses, our distresses, our sorrows, our pains, our afflictions, our transgressions, our oppressions, our all—yet He was submissive to all of this, just as a lamb that was led to the slaughter, He did not open His mouth complaining—you will find a more detailed explanation of this farther in the book. He was separated from His Father's love and presence while in this world of darkness. He literally felt and experienced the pain and agony from the demons of hell and why did He do this; it was because of His love for me and His love for you, that we might have a chance to accept His salvation plan for us. My Father tells me to ask the question—"who has believed, who has trusted, who has relied upon faith in Me, who has accepted what I have brought to all, who has received My love and are letting it show through them to others"?

I accepted the Lord as my personal Saviour at the age of seventeen. My old way of life before I believed in Him is completely in the past—I consider it as a changing of clothes that has been thrown away—this being a once-for-all decision when I receive His gift of salvation, this being a daily conscious commitment. I put on this new role, headed in a new direction, and have a new way of thinking that the Holy Spirit gives me.

I married at the age of twenty-four, yet a part of this devil junk that had been tormenting me, followed me right on through until I determined to really take my hands off of my life; giving it all into His hands; not holding back anything but releasing everything, and I mean everything, into His hands (just because we have received and accepted His salvation does not mean that everything comes automatic—we have to realize or become aware of the things the enemy has and is still putting on us and give them everyone to our Lord and Master; ask and He will take them all off us)—then Praise God!!! He lifted it all off from me!!! I just gave my all to Him, then He took my burdens and cares, wrapped His loving arms around me and gave me a new place in His home!!! Oh, how He loves for us to give it all to Him so that He can lavish His all on us!!! Jesus is alive and my past is dead, I am forgiven. He literally opens heaven's gates to me and pours His blessings upon me!!! Glory, glory, it feels so very, very good to be set free. Don't try hiding anything from Him. Why are you so troubled and in so much fear; let every fear you might have, or have ever had, just melt in His presence. Let the love He places inside your heart be far more than yours alone. Let it be a love that is never going to die because He has given it to you, that He might show Himself to you and through you—again I say, in ways such as your mind cannot understand.

Jesus is the Lord of all, I have been redeemed!!! He is my Joy!!! He will never let go of my hand but will always be right there with me and for me!!! He gives me Freedom!!! He gives me Righteousness!!! He gives me Holiness!!! Holiness is the only life that He can really and truly bless, so I must stay under His blessed shelter that His shed blood purchased for me, that no shame of the past life will ever be seen or felt anymore!!! I find it so very difficult to come up with the words to even begin to explain or describe what He has and is doing for me (words seem so very, very insignificant), **it has to be experienced.** It is so very great, exciting, joyful, comforting, loving, peaceful and strengthening!!! I do not want anything else; just want to please Him all the time, in everything I do; looking to hear Him say to me—"well done, you have been obedient to Me"—that is worth it all.

* * *

Table of Contents

In the Beginning

Greetings in the name of Jesus Christ our Lord and Saviour.

My name is Leon Coates and life for me began on December 22, 1928 in a very small, secluded country home, near Shorterville, Alabama. I was the second of three boys born into this family. Livelihood during these years was an extreme struggle with survival being the name of the game.

When I was five years old my family moved across the Chattahoochee River to a place several miles south of Fort Gaines, Georgia, and I have lived in this area since. I started and finished school at Clay County Schools in Fort Gaines. During the time I was in the third grade, my daddy died as the results of an accident.

My mother was thirty-two years of age at the time of his death but she chose to remain unmarried and put herself to the task of rearing her three sons, giving her life to this responsibility.

I think when I learned to read I started trying to read the Bible. I was taught at an early age about what was right and what was wrong, was carried to church, was trained and led at home, as best they knew how.

At the age of seventeen I accepted the Lord as my personal Saviour, and my name was placed on a Baptist church roll. Immediately the church started putting me in places of responsibility, which I was not ready for but tried to take it seriously. As I look back, I see pride stepping in and being a hindrance to the Lord working through me. Churches, please be careful about when and who you put in places of responsibilities. In a very short time I was teaching, leading the song service, deacon, and then chairman of the deacon board, among other things—as I said I took all this seriously, and the Lord blessed.

In January 1953, I married the girl with whom I spent over forty-six years—we had a very good marriage, and all I remember of our time together are very pleasant thoughts. We gave birth to three wonderful children—one daughter, two sons, who are all living and doing great.

Included in these years were many trials and victories with God becoming more real to us as time passed by.

We lived one mile from the Baptist church which we spent many years of our life participating in. The people that were in this church were local people, with many of them being buried in the church cemetery in passing years. Some of the children of some of these people are still in that church.

When the time came to build the new and present building, I was elected to be the chairman of the building committee. The building was completed but soon afterward, the Lord moved my family and me to another church.

All this time I was asking pastor after pastor questions which none would or could answer. The Lord told me in later years that they could not give me answers, because they had not experienced what I was asking about. He says that a person cannot tell you about something that they have not experienced themselves, particularly with any power (they might tell you about what they had been taught or heard, but would be powerless in their presentation).

Time goes by and all the children graduate and go their separate ways. At the present I am the proud "PA" of six grandchildren, with some of them having graduated and going their separate and various ways.

*   *   *

Changing Times and Lives

O n March 17, 1999, Bobbie, my wife of over forty-six years, went to be with the Lord, permanently. To say the least, this changed my way of life immediately. This seemed to be causing me to lose the meaning of life. I tried going to bed for three or four nights following her death, but could not stay there, so it resulted in my sitting on a recliner for two full years, before trying the bed again. Two years to the month, almost to the night, I tried the bed again and the Lord blessed me to remain there and use the bed from that time on.

Many nights, during the time of sitting on the recliner the Lord and I would talk all night long—when coming time to get up in the morning, I would arise feeling very rested, ready to go. The Lord would talk to me and give me visions of many things, (some of which I will share farther into this book) causing Him to become so very real to me. Life began to become very meaningful, and yes, very exciting. I was finding something so worthwhile to live for. He was show-ing Himself to me as my Messiah, Avenger, Comforter, Potentate, Strength, Wisdom, Provider, and Blood Covenant, among other things. In April following Bobbie's death in March, I was in church, sitting on the front pew alone, interceding as the Lord was telling me to do—He tells me and shows me so very many things. There is no way to tell you all that He has said and done with me since then.

He has begun to send me around to various churches in different sections of the country. One morning He told me He wanted me to go to a certain church in Dothan, Alabama. I told Him, "Lord, I do not so much as know that this church exists", but before the day was over He had me talking to the pastor of this church, by just doing His thing—all I did was act on what He told me. I went to this church, and on the third trip there the pastor told me to go ahead. I was on the front seat so all I had to do was turn around and the Lord took control and began to speak through me, using this vessel and my voice, but I do not remember a word that was said, I could see what was happening, with my eyes, but did not know what He was saying. At one point everyone slipped out of their shoes, and shortly everyone was coming up front. When He stopped talking I asked Him, "Lord what is going on"? Then as I was turning around to face all the people that were behind me, who were all standing at this time, but by the time I had completed the turn, everyone was on the floor, worshipping and praising the Lord—I have never seen this happen before or since then. The Lord tells me that He has His people ready for a supernatural, spiritual, revival (and did He!!!!). The pastor stopped things and would not let them go any farther. This was the pattern of all the churches that He sent me to. After sending me to several churches, He tells me that the *results* of my being obedient to Him and doing what He told me to do was not my responsibility, but His. He says that the pastors are so jealous they will not let a spiritual move start in their churches because it was not coming through them (or some well known or educated source) but through someone else, particularly a laymen, as they look at it. What a shameful situation—is this any different from Jesus' time in dealing with the priest, (leaders of religion), I think not. I find that mainly the people are hungry for the Lord and His moving. The people absorb His teaching and ways, like a sponge absorbing water, yet they are being hindered from the reality of the moving of the Father, by the leaders. If you will remember, it was the priest (the religious leaders) that very pointedly instigated and pushed the crucifixion of Jesus on the cross.

* * *

New Beginnings in Life

Several days after the funeral, I was asked by an evangelist friend from Dothan, Alabama, to go to Hong Kong with him, on a missionary trip. I quickly told him I do not want to go to Hong Kong—he asked me to talk to the Lord about it and I promised him I would—to get him off my back. Some nights later, while sitting on my recliner, the Lord gave me a vision, letting me know He wanted me to go to Hong Kong— (He showed me in a group of people, being His vessel, and He was leading all the people into a spiritual revival. When I asked Him if this would be manifested if I did not go to Hong Kong, He very firmly said no)—so I went to Hong Kong during the first week of August 1999. The whole trip, including the vision in telling me to go, was a series of miracles. We serve such an awesome, awesome God!!!

I was on a team of six workers—we had been assigned a church to work through before we got to Hong Kong, but the heads of the mission had some friends in Hawaii that wanted a church, so they took ours and gave it to them, leaving us with the team group meeting in a building that was Chinese government sponsored—mainly a gathering place for children to come and play. No adults were present except the staff for the first three days. On this particular morning I was left standing in the meeting room of this building, because the rest of the team had gone into rooms. While standing there some teenagers came by and I was witnessing to them—one could speak very little English, so the Lord used her to relay on to the others (who accepted Him as their Lord and Saviour first), leaving this one until last. She was very thorough in her searching before she finally said yes. Immediately after accepting the Lord as her Saviour she left, leaving me alone. When I stood up I became aware that I was in the building alone— the team and staff had left without letting me know anything about their leaving. While talking to the Lord about the situation, I was aware that as I spoke, one word I was still here, but before I spoke another word, I was across town, standing in the doorway looking at the rest of team. GLORY, GLORY, GLORY, WHAT AN AWESOME, WONDERFUL GOD WE SERVE!!!!! In a moment, in the twinkling of an eye it happened—OUR GOD IS SUCH AN AWESOME GOD!!!!!!!!!!!!!

He takes pleasure in doing these kinds of things with His children. He told me all He needed was for me to be obedient and open to Him—as long as I would be yielded and obedient to Him He would use me whenever, wherever, however, He so desired and needed. He has shown me time and again that He means what He says and says what He means. I have stopped being surprised at what He would do and how He would do it, but continue to walk in amazement all the time. He is such an awesome, loving, and caring Person. I thank Him for His loving kindness and tender mercies that flow from Him so freely to everyone that will receive them and love Him for Who He is. Thank you Father, for the peace that goes beyond all understanding, into the depths of Your love and graces. I have never known a fellowship, a relationship, such as this in my lifetime. I truly thank You for Your nearness, the intimate, the overwhelming, and powerful closeness, that prevails all the time as I talk and walk and live in this fellowship with You. You too, can enjoy this kind of a relationship with Father God if you will be open and obedient.

It seems every way I turned He brought about His miracles to carry me on and lift me up. I was asked to teach a Sunday school class by some of the members of a church. In Hong Kong, you walk down the sidewalk and when you come to openings or doorways in the buildings, you go in and go up the stairs or get on the elevator. As we got off the elevator that particular morning, we stepped out into a very small room, and waited until time for Sunday school to start. When starting time came the others got up and went somewhere—no one told me where to go, and everyone of them knew that I was suppose to teach a class—so here I am alone again. I had no idea which way to go, or what to do, because no one told me anything. About that time a guy got off the elevator which I was standing very near. He could speak a little English, so we spoke and I told him why I was there. He told me this was his first time to visit this church, but he told me to go with him. I followed him right into a certain room, which was the correct room, and he got a folding chair and told me to sit down, and he sat down right beside me, this being the class I was suppose to teach (the group of youth was waiting so the Lord put me at the right place).

I was invited out the following night to supper at a restaurant by a girl I met at church, and when I met her at the eating place, she said for us to wait a minute for someone who turned out to be the guy that had helped me so much at church. The Lord has His purpose and timing for doing all things, so this was His timing for the leading of this guy to accept and believe on Him, as his personal Saviour. We left him happy and with purpose in life, now and for the future.

The evangelist and I stayed over a couple of days after the others had returned home—we wanted to see more of Hong Kong, but did not get to because the people there kept us busy. The pastor of the church we went to, invited us out to his apartment on Tuesday night before we left on Wednesday—we had a great time with him, his family, and others he had invited in.

We were told that approximately ninety percent of the people there lived in apartments—everywhere you look you see some kind of high-rise apartment complex—I was told that the older apartments were around two hundred square feet, for the family to live in—the newer ones consisted of around four hundred square feet living area, so you can see that they were not blessed with an over abundance of space.

Even amid miracles being manifested, the enemy and his forces are always present, trying to do his dirt, but praise God, he just has to move on when the Father does what He wants done (He needs obedient and empty and yielded vessels and He will do His thing). There are ninety-six fifteen minute sequences in a twenty-four hour period—how many of these do you put aside everything else and just spend with Him? He wants and longs for the time of intimacy being spent with Him, where He can talk with you and you can talk with Him. In very simple language He desires and wants you to know Him—not just know of Him or about Him. We have to truly know Him to be an overcomer, and overcomers are the ones who will be included in the number that will make up the bride for Jesus Christ. <u>He says many hang around the cross, but few hang on the cross.</u>

The greatest power that God gives to man is the *power of choice*. Put it into action, meditate, apply the Word. He made each and everyone of us vessels of choice—*we are making choices* all the time, whether we are aware of it or not, whether intentional or unintentional, whether right or wrong. That is the way that God made us. He chose to set His system up on this basis—He made these choices with us in mind and He desires and wants His created beings to have intimate fellowship with Him—He wants you to choose Him. To please Him we have to do and use His ways and means. He even let Lucifer make use of this method and make choices all his own—He allows man to do the same, whether right or contrariwise He still honors each person's choosing—whether a person chooses to go to hell or whether he chooses to go be with the Lord in heaven. God says He wants possessors not mere professors. He wants people to really know Him, not just know about or of Him— you have to know Him to be overcomers—His bride is made up of overcomers not just professors.

The reason churches are putting up with so much hell is because they are listening to it. The first step to resisting the devil is, *do not listen to him*—spend your time fitting every loose thought and emotions and impulse into the structure of life shaped by Christ.

Choose whether you will live serving Him and being a citizen of His kingdom, or whether you will serve the worldly kingdom. Joshua tells us to "choose you this day whom you will serve or follow". (Josh 24:15)

* * *

Another Miracle

There were many other miracles that were manifested-
during these days in Hong Kong. I would like to share
a final one with you.

We have finally boarded the plane to return home, this
was around dinner time on Wednesday the ninth of August,
I believe is the correct date. After all were seated, the pilot's
voice sounded over the speaker system saying that we would
be flying to a height of forty thousand feet plus, before leveling off for flight. I remember thinking, Lord we will be
around eight miles high—I have never been that high before.
The Lord placed me by the window right behind the wing on
the left side of the plane, the emergency exit door was right
in front of me. I did not do a whole lot of looking while on
the ascension because we were flying through lots of clouds.
After leveling off in flight, I started looking out the window,
the Lord drew my attention to the wing. Now, I am quite
mechanically minded, and as my attention was drawn to the
wing area, I noticed that the engine toward the end of the
wing was not still, it was trembling and shaking on the wing.
It was not difficult for me to understand that something was
not just right, and here we are eight miles high over the

Pacific Ocean. Immediately I began to talk to the Lord about the situation—I sensed no fear whatsoever, but I knew something was going to happen unless the condition was corrected, and how was it going to be corrected eight miles high, over the Pacific Oceans? I told the Lord that this was not the way I was suppose to meet You (no reply), then I said that there was over four hundred people on this plane and very few of them are ready to meet You (no reply)—He just nudged me in my spirit, and I knew what He wanted me to do, so I looked out at what was the faulty area and spoke to it in Jesus name. Yes, almost as if you would throw a light toggle switch the engine stopped trembling and shaking completely, and as far as I know it has not trembled or shaken since then. There is no greater God than my Father—there is none other!!!!

And yes, I understand why He put His vessel in that particular seat, at this particular time—His timing is precise.

He told me sometime later, that had the engine fallen from the plane, it would have taken part of the wing with it, causing a fatal crash—WHAT A LOVING FATHER!

Jeremiah tells us to call upon the Lord and He will answer, showing us great and mighty things, that we know not. Jesus tells us in Mat 7:7 to "ask and it shall be given you; seek and you will find; knock and it shall be opened unto you".

Jesus is our personal miracle worker—He gives us what we need, what we want, and what we desire. Know that God will do it for you—make the devil obey you—cancer, sickness, or anything he puts on you, by speaking in the knowledge of authority in the word, by faith with God. If you want kingdom power you must live under and by kingdom rules—think in your spirit, shut off your mind.

This happened shortly after dinner or lunch time but a short time later we flew into the night. I think all the passengers went to sleep shortly after getting into darkness, but do you think I could sleep after what had just transpired? No, I am wide awake looking around at all the others sleeping. The stewardess came by and pulled my window shade down but sometime later I raised it and looked outside. The lights on the plane showed the wing and the engine, which had been *heavenly* corrected of whatever was wrong with it.

Some minutes later I looked outside again and what do you think I saw? There setting on the wing of that plane was the big star dipper (all seven stars), if I could have gotten my arm out through my window I could have caught the first star on the handle of the dipper in my hand. I considered that along the way somewhere, the plane and the dipper could have aligned in position to cause it to look like this (we are eight miles high), but, no, not for a full two hours time—I kept check of time, and again I say, no. I elbowed my evangelist friend and told him to look—he did and went right back to sleep. Then later we flew into day again—my evangelist friend, after awakening from his sleep, turned to me and said, "Brother Leon, I don't believe I would tell that"— immediately the Lord told me firmly in my spirit, "Yes you do tell it, I did it and you tell it"——HE SEES ALL—HE KNOWS ALL—HE DOES ALL—GLORY!!!!!!!!!! GLORY!!!!!!!!!!!!!

As I said before, He wants to do all these good things for His children but He must have obedience and yieldedness first and then He is endless in what He does——

HOW REAL——HOW VERY REAL HE IS!!!!!!!!!!!!!

Needless to say, we finished the trip *blessed* and very much in His care. Gen 22:17-18—*That in blessing I will bless you, and in multiplying I will multiply your seeds as the stars of the heaven, and as the sand which is upon the sea shore; and your seed shall possess the gate of your enemy. And in your seed shall all the nations of the earth be blessed; because you have obeyed my voice.*

By the way, at the close of the weeks mission work all

the workers came together for a farewell gathering, during which each group presented the results of their ministry efforts for the week. This was presented church by church, with our time being at the tail end of the line. When our leader gave the report, the number of decisions from our situation, was almost as much as all the churches put together or total of all churches. I continue to say, *give all to God* and He will never quit returning of Himself to you. *Jn 4:35— Well, I am telling you to open your eyes and take a good look at what is right in front of you. These Samaritans fields are ripe. It is harvest time. (The Message).* The Lord says— Truly the harvest is very plentiful but the laborers are few!!!!

* * *

Our Lord's Agony
for You and Me

Please consider and study the following chapters of scriptures as you go into this experience:
Mat 26-28   Mk 14-16   Lk 22-24   Jn 17-21

Let me at this time share one of the experiences that my Father took me through. This was on Easter morning of 2000, during the night hours of the morning (I do not remember the exact hours). My Lord wakes me and tells me He is going to take me through the trial hours and on into the crucifixion of His Son Jesus.

He told me that He wanted me to feel a portion of the agony and pain that His Son went through and experienced for you and me. He gave me a detailed vision of each step of the trial, and particularly each step of the painful consequences that Jesus went through. It would be almost impossible for me (Leon) to justify the details and description of each, so I am asking my Father to relay them to me so that I can pass on what He desires in this.

Please remember why this was happening—it was not

for Him, but it was for you and me. Can your mind comprehend, or even begin to comprehend such love as this? Keep this ever present on your mind as we go into what He has for us to see, and yes, let Him cause you to literally feel in your spirit, the actual agonies and pain that is being incurred, remembering that this agony and pain that should have been ours, and He is taking it for us. He suffered this so we could have the opportunity of believing and accepting Him as our personal Savior and Master++++My God, what love+++++

We will start at Gethsemane where Jesus spent hours praying that night. He took Peter, James, and John part way to where He was going to pray alone—He prayed an hour, then coming to where they were, He found them sleeping. He had already told Peter earlier that he would deny Him three times before the rooster crows at dawn, now He finds him sleeping, and not being able to pray with Him for just one full hour—asking him "Can't you stick it out with Me a single hour?" (The Message). He left them a second time, going and praying, and when He came back a second time, he again found them sleeping—this time He let them sleep on, and went a third time to pray. When He came back the final time He asked, "Are you going to sleep on and make a night of it? My time is up, the Son of Man is about to be handed over into the hands of sinners. Get up!! Let's get going!! My betrayer is here." (The Message). Judas brought a gang with him to take Jesus by force to the high priest. Jesus was betrayed by one and the others scattered and left Him—with Peter following at a long distance (and he did deny Him, even to the place of cursing and swearing, just like Jesus said he would and at the timing He said, too).

He was taken before Caiaphas, the Chief Priest, where the religious scholars and leaders had assembled. All these religious leaders did all they could to find fault with Him, using false witnesses and false charges, but when they said they had evidence enough for death, they began spitting in

His face and banging Him around—slapping Him and telling Him to *Prophesy, Messiah, and tell us who hit you that time.*

Already, look at the agony of rejection, by religion, by his apostles, by seemingly all—even those that had lived these months with Him—those that received many miracles from Him—those that He had spoke and showed love and only love to. To sum it all up, here is Jesus all alone, no one coming to His aid or offering help to Him. The agony had surely begun—are you still with Him? My Father kept me by His side through it all, that I might see and feel just a glimpse of the reality of what is going on. He only let me feel and experience just a very small portion (or extent) of the actual crushing and devastating pain and agony that was given and laid on Jesus.

If you, at this time, will look at the situation from man's view, you would surely say that Jesus had failed miserably in His mission on earth. But not so, look at the victory that He is bringing about—it does appear that there is no such thing as victory on Jesus' part, but seems the victory is going the other way. It surely looks as if the devil is having a heyday, by using people to do his deeds. He thinks he is finally destroying the Messiah the Anointed One, the One that he had spent thousand of years and means to stop (was he fooled, as usual?). You see, God's ways are not our ways, His thoughts are not our thoughts, His wisdom is not our wisdom, His plans are not our plans. He knows what He is doing, it is obvious that man's wisdom is not His wisdom, but God's wisdom is ours for the asking and *seeking. (Jas 1:5 tells us that we are to "ask boldly, believingly, without a second thought" (The Message).* He wants us to be instructed by (*Let the Word of Christ have the run of the house giving it plenty of room in your lives. Instruct and direct one another using good common sense. And sing, sing your hearts out to God! Let every detail in your lives—words, actions, whatever—be done in the name of the*

Master, Jesus, thanking God the Father every step of the way—Col 3:16-17 (The Message)—encompassed by and led by and through His Wisdom, not the wisdom of man.

Next Jesus was placed before Pilate, the governor, who began asking Him questions to which He made no reply, really impressing the governor, who wanted to release Him and let Him go free because he found no substantual evidence against Him. Religion was so strong in the people that they were at the point of starting a riot, and Pilate did not want that, so he gave them the choice of releasing Jesus or one called Barabbas, who was a criminal with a death sentence hanging on him—religion chose to release the criminal and put Jesus to open shame and death.

The agony of rejection is being followed now by much physical abuse and torment. Pilate had Jesus stripped of His clothes that covered His back and then had Him tied to the whipping post. Each lash that was applied, literally stripped flesh from all the way across His back, leaving it open where you are looking at the bones (Oh, my God, what brutal and agonizing pain and torment). The strips of flesh (some are loose and fall to the floor and other places) that are not pulled loose are still hanging from His back and body—I am looking at the bare bones during this time—the flesh is mutilated beyond your imagination—very little still on His back.

I am asking Him during these times, *Lord why are you doing this*, why don't you just call the legions of angels to stop this. Every time I ask the answer is the same, *"I love you this much"*—it does not matter when I ask, He takes the time and effort to give me the same answer. Are you still with Him? My God, My God, what love.

By this time, it is quite evident that a strong man would be overcome or subdued, but not our Jesus. The flesh is being cut from His bones, the blood is freely running everywhere (His blood is still running freely everywhere for you and me). All the times that we turned our back on Him, that we refused to be obedient to Him, that we did things that we wanted to do to satisfy our flesh and ways of thinking, and even saying that we will get to Him in a more available time—He went through the rejection and the hell, the literal destruction of His body, the shedding of His blood, the mutilating of the flesh, the pain, just for you and me. He will forgive us for all the excuses and rebellion when we come to Him in reality asking His forgiveness.

Isaiah 52:14 prophecies (*For many, the Servant of God became an object of horror, many were astonished at Him), His face and His whole appearance were marred more than any man's, and His form beyond that of the sons of men."* *Amplified version.* Isaiah prophesied and saw this, in his spirit, many hundreds of years before it happened. According to what the Lord showed me, it is still the most accurate description that we have ever had available. Sometimes it takes hundreds and thousands of years for prophecy to be completely fulfilled, but it is and will be manifested, to the detail, in full accuracy.

Jesus does not, at any time, through all this, let His love for us waiver. You see, He was in this all alone—even the Father turned His back on Jesus, that His purpose and will might be carried out for man, because that was the way that it had to be. Oh God, what agony, what pain (think of the agony of rejection and pain of all people throughout eternity being laid upon Him). What is your present picture of Him now?

People seemingly are endless in their sinning, they take Jesus now and throw a purple (scarlet) robe on Him (this standing for dignity and worn by Roman officers of rank), they have no mercy on the One Who is Mercy. Now they place a crown of thorns on His head (each thorn was approximately two inches long being very sharp) and forced it down that the thorns may stick into His head all around, then handing Him a staff, a stick. A battalion of soldiers had came in (according to history this would be six hundred or more men)—these soldiers, who came in for the purpose of mocking and jeering at Jesus, started marching and circling around Jesus, mocking, jeering, and making fun of Him— taking the stick and hitting the thorn crown (each time He was hit, it drove the thorns deeper, agitating even more) on His head, and spitting upon Him; you see, I am still standing there by Him. Would you please try to imagine at the present, just what the appearance of Jesus was after over six hundred men had continually spit upon Him and probably more than one time, with the purple (scarlet) robe becoming stuck to His body with blood, His head swelling because of the thorns that are protruding into it, His face also swelling and distorted, caused by the slappings and the literal hittings by the soldiers and also the people of religion—He suffered even for all these, too. As Isaiah said He was marred beyond visage (not recognizable). His appearance was so disfigured beyond that of any man and His form marred beyond human likeness (NIV). **He loved us so much (even at this point He continues to tell me, I love you this much, will you give Me your all)**—have we allowed or chosen this kind of love to be instilled in and controlling us? Might I call your attention to the pictures of Jesus on the cross that we might have in our possession or have seen other places, during our lifetime. I would truly say that I have not seen one that portrays the true facts of the actual process and condition as it really was, that shows us the actual results as He hung on the cross, but we very much need to keep this before our eyes at all times, that our appreciation for Him might be kept intensified, and that we can walk in this love more freely.

Now they take Jesus, they pull the purple (scarlet) robe off Him, (with strips of flesh stuck to it and being pulled off) and put His clothes back on the mutilated body, and lay the cross upon His shoulders (think of the shredded flesh that the weight of the heavy cross is being applied to). I do not know what kind of wood the cross was made of, whether it was green wood or dry wood, but one thing I am sure of is that it had considerable weight either way (weighing many pounds), this being all put upon a mutilated, deformed body to bear the weight of. The beating or the crown of thorns could either one have disabled a strong well man, but here it is all put on the same person, with Him accepting it and carrying it all for you and me. He did this that we would not have to go through it, of necessity, ourselves—**He loved us that much and He continues to tell me so**—each and everyone of us were there present at His side whether we are really aware of it or not.

The shock, the exhaustion, the pain, the mental anguish, the agonizing rejection, the wrong exalting over right, was enough to kill several strong men. Jesus knew He had to succeed in this and through this in order that His love could be given to everyone. How can we comprehend such an awesome, amazing love as this? Because He was victorious this **love** is available to each and—all.

As we reached Golgotha they took the cross and laid it on the ground, then they took Jesus and stripped all His clothes off Him except a loin cloth. If you will remember at this time they cast lots (they literally threw dice to see who got His clothes, but would not tear or cut, that prophecy might be fulfilled). Finally they laid Jesus on the cross and nailed Him to it, using enormous nails or spikes in each hand and the feet, then lifted Him on the cross and dropped it into a hole with a downward force causing extreme strain, pain, and shock. Think about the extreme pressure that was put on the areas where the nails or spikes were. Now, are you beginning to see how satan takes full use of the opportunity to let his anger and hatred be expressed against Jesus and our Father God. You see, the Father cast him (satan) out, so he is enjoying doing everything that he possibly can or is being allowed to do. It really seems that all the rebellion of the religious leaders, all the rejection of the ones that walked with Him, all the pain and suffering, was programmed through satanic and demonic opposition—cannot you imagine what a joyful time satan and his demons were having? Even when His Father turned His back on Him (**He still says I love you this much**), because the Father could not look at the sin that was being laid upon Jesus, His Son. Don't you, at this time, get a very small gist of what is prevailing in the life of Jesus—He is being separated from His Father God— this has to be a time of darkness and feeling of utter lostness and despair. Oh Jesus, Oh Jesus, will we ever be brought to the realization of the love that You gave to each and everyone of us?

All I could do was stand and take account of what He wanted me to feel and see. Dear one, words are not sufficient to bring out the reality of what transpired during this time—and please know that it was done just for you and me. Jesus did not need it, the Father did not need it, the Holy Spirit did not need it—it was you and I that needed it—what **love, what Holy Love**, was poured out that we could be given a new life to live with Him—preparing for the time when He will come to receive us or get His Bride. Dear beloved one, you do not get these benefits through work, you do not get them through organization, you do not get them except one way—that way is by reaching out in faith to Him, no one else, just Him, partaking and receiving what He has and wants to bestow upon you—it is a gift, nothing you can earn, He has already paid for it in full, just accept it all in Jesus name.

Let us think too, when the clothes were taken off His body, that strips of flesh that had dried and stuck to the robe, was pulled loose and came off with it. Very little of His body was left unmutilated—this is what was hanging on the cross, not what you see in most of the pictures we look at. Now, will you begin to visualize the accurate picture of the reality of the crucifixion and what Jesus bore for you and me—that is the reason He says He wants possessors rather than mere professors. God wants you to know Him rather than know of or about Him.

I have already told you that He wanted me to feel a portion of what He is feeling. The majority of the places that He sends me gives me a feeling of anguish or suffering, sometimes both. This indicates to me or tells me that He is hurting because of the spiritual condition of the people involved in the particular situation. Surely this shows that He has no reason to be pleased with this. Rather or quite seldom I will go to places that I will feel His joy in reality because He would be pleased with what would be happening there. Also you can see the reality of "wide is the way that leads to destruction and many there be who enters into it." On the other hand you see that, "narrow is the way that leads into life everlasting with God and few there be that enters therein". He tell us these things, yet people still make choices to go their ways which are contrariwise to His; still Jesus so lovingly went through all the agony of rejection and torment of sufferings of the body and Spirit to make a way of escape for every individual, not just a few, but for everyone, because everyone is given the freedom of choice.

May I share some words the Lord sends to me:

IT IS IN THE VALLEY THAT I GROW

I have so very much to learn
And my growth is sometimes slow,
Sometimes I need the mountaintops,
But it is in the valleys that I grow.
I do not always understand

Why things happen as they do,
But I am very sure of one thing,
My Lord will see me through.
My little valleys are nothing
When I picture Christ on the cross
He went through the valley of death,
His victory was satan's loss.
Forgive me Lord, for complaining
When I am feeling so very low.
Just give me a gentle reminder
That it is in the valleys I grow.
Continue to strengthen me, Lord
And use my life each day
To share your love with others.
Thank you for my valleys, Lord,
For this one thing I know,
The mountaintops are glorious
But it is in the valleys I grow.
If I always stayed on mountain top
And never experienced pain,
I would never appreciate God's love
And would be living in vain.
Sometimes life seems hard to bear,
Full of sorrow, trouble and woe,
That it is then I have to remember
it is in the valleys that I grow.
!!!!!!Well, Glory to the Most Holy One!!!!!!

May I again call your attention (it is difficult to express strongly enough), to the mockery and verbal abuse (along with the physical), that was thrown on Jesus continually during this time. Now think about yourself when someone just gives you a naughty look or says something crosswise to you—what attitude and action do you take in dealing with this—is it the same that Jesus gave for us in all that

He went through?

According to record, Jesus was crucified at nine o'clock in the morning, with the soldiers and the leaders of religion constantly mocking and throwing accusations at Him. Can you picture or put yourself in this situation and still say with Him, "Father forgive them for they don't know what they are doing?"

Around noontime the sky began turning dark and stayed that way—later Jesus said "I thirst", then even later He says "It is finished, it is done, Father have your way". The curtain in the temple was rent or torn apart, from top to bottom, (signifying that you do not have to go through a priest anymore, to be able to reach Him, but you can approach the Lord personally—as an individual go into His presence, because Jesus became our high Priest). Heb 4:14-15—*Now that we know what we have—Jesus, this great High Priest with ready access to God—let us not let it slip through our fingers. We do not have a priest who is out of touch with our reality. He has been through weaknesses and testing, experienced it all—all but the sin. So let us walk right up to Him and get what He is so ready to give. Take the mercy, accept the help. Heb 8:1—In essence, we have just such a high priest, authoritative right alongside God, conducting worship in the one true sanctuary built by God. (The Message).* There was a great earthquake, rocks were split, tombs were opened, and the dead came to life, and after Jesus' resurrection, they left the tombs or graves and entered the holy city, appearing to many.

Look at victory, satan thought he was having all kinds of victory, but it was his loss—Jesus through the cross brought victory, satan has been a defeated foe ever since the cross and we are the winning participants of this victory. "Glory, Glory, Glory"

Jn 5:26—For as the Father has life in Himself; so has He given to His Son to have life in Himself. God is an eternal living God, not a dead god, He is a God of the living, not the dead—Jesus took sin with Him into the grave, but when He arose (resurrection) He left sin there and came forth a new life, bringing God down to us—you are dead to sin and alive to God, that is what Jesus did for us. God wants His children to know this and walk with Him in a living eternal life, experiencing the living life to the fullest in Him. (*Jn 10:10—A thief is only there to steal and kill and destroy. I came so they can have real and eternal life, more and better life than they ever dreamed of—The Message*). This means that you must not give sin the time of the day, or even run errands for sin, that are connected with the old life, but we are to do God's bidding in living His way. We cannot let sin tell us how to live, for we are dead to sin, but living in the freedom of God. (*Rom 8:5-8—Those who think they can do it on their own end up obsessed with measuring their own moral muscle but never get around to exercising it in real life. Those who trust God's action in them find that God's Spirit is in them—living and breathing God! Obsession with self in these matters is a dead end; attention to God leads us out into the open, into a spacious life. Focusing on the self is the opposite of focusing on God. Anyone completely absorbed in self ignores God, ends up thinking more about self than God. That person ignores who God is and what He is doing. And God isn't pleased at being ignored—The Message*). When giving yourself to the ways of God, freedom never quits, so choose to live openly in His freedom, that He openly gives to us as believers.

One other thing I want you to see, when the Roman captain (along with the other soldiers) there with Jesus, saw what had happened when He stopped breathing and gave up the ghost, he honored God saying, "This man was innocent—a good man—He has to be the Son of God". Jesus makes the difference wherever, whenever, however, He goes. Can you think of anyone else that can began to compare with Jesus—I think not? Tell your mind to shut up and let your spirit do your thinking—the spirit will not mislead you—the mind can be used by the enemy to lead you astray and cause you to think contrariwise thoughts. *Jn 7:13-14—Don't look for shortcuts to God. The market is flooded with surefire, easygoing formulas for a successful life that can be practiced in your spare time. Do not fall for that stuff, even though crowds of people do. The way of life—to God!—is vigorous and requires total attention— The Message*). Spend time in intimacy with the Father, and He will cause you to be able to do this.

What the Father says about His Son:

> "As a sheep led to slaughter,
> And quiet as a lamb being sheared,
> He was silent, saying nothing.
> He was mocked and put down,
> Never got a fair trial,
> But who now can count his kin
> Since he has been taken from the earth?"
> Heaven is My throne room;
> I rest My feet on earth.
> So what kind of house
> Will you build Me?" says God.
> Where I can get away and relax?
> It is already built, and I built it."!
> My Son! My very own Son!
> Today I celebrate You!"
> (The Message—Acts 8:32-33; 7:49-50)

> He appeared in a human body,
> Was proved right by the invisible Spirit,
> Was seen by angels.
> He was proclaimed among all kinds of peoples,

Believed in all over the world,
Taken up into heavenly glory.
(The Message—1 Tim 3:16)

Well, since you have this new freedom, (*Jn 8:36—So if the Son sets you free, you are free through and through—The Message*), does that mean that you can live any old way or do anything that comes to mind? Absolutely not—No, No, No—you know that if you give in to just one act of the old life that calls for another, and still more another's, so you have to let the dead remain dead, and do the things that causes this new life to become more and more evident and real in your life.

(*Eph 3:20—God can do anything, you know—far more than you could imagine or guess or request in your wildest dreams! He does it not by pushing us around but by working within us, his Spirit deeply and gently within us.—The Message*), Let His power flow through you—be a vessel that will be an opening for Him in whatever way He so desires.

Our old way of life was nailed to the cross with Christ, conquering death, knowing that we were included in His life saving resurrection. (*Col 2:13-15—When you were stuck in your old sin-dead life, you were incapable of responding to God. God brought you alive—right along with Christ! Think of it! All sins forgiven, the slate wiped clean, that old arrest warrant canceled and nailed to Christ's Cross. He stripped all the spiritual tyrants in the universe of their sham authority at the Cross and marched them naked through the streets—The Message*). Death does not have dominion over us any longer because Jesus loved us, being all that we could not be, for us, that we can be as we are. You might want to study Romans chapter 6 and 7 here, at this point.

You worked hard for sin all your life and all that you have stored up (for a pension) is death—but the new life, the God-life, the eternal life with God, has been delivered to us by Jesus Christ, our beloved Master, and you have eternal life stored up for you. When Jesus Christ died he took all the old life into the tomb and left it there, so you are free to marry a resurrection life and have children of faith for God—He took sin down into the grave with Him, after coming back to life He brought God down to earth to us. You are feeling birth pains all along, the problems that confront you in this life are mere opportunities for your God to show Himself in and through you, causing you to become stronger through each and everyone. Jesus made things right in this life of contradictions, where we want to serve God with all our heart and mind and desire to do things so differently. In His Son Jesus God took on the human condition in order to set it right once and for all—so simply embrace what His Spirit is doing for and in you. Do not think that you can do it on your own—let God's living and breathing Spirit, which is in you, give you wisdom and strength to get it done. God's Spirit touches our spirit and lets us know who we really are—brother and sister, I am saying according to the holy Word of God, that you will surely need all this to confront life in the not to far future—so please know God as your Father and not just know of Him or about Him.

Because of Jesus Christ there is nothing living or dead, angelic or demonic, high or low, today or tomorrow, thinkable or unthinkable, large or small, and I mean absolutely *nothing*, that can come between or stand between you and God's love for you—truly, truly, make use of this while you can and opportunity avails. *Who would dare even to point a finger? The one Who died for us—Who was raised to life for us!—is in the presence of God at this very moment sticking up for us. Do you think anyone is going to be able to drive a wedge between us and Christ's love for us?*

There is no way! Not trouble, not hard times, not hatred, not hunger, not homelessness, not bullying threats, not back-stabbing, not even the worst sins listed in Scriptures; "They

*kill us in cold blood because they hate you. We're sitting
ducks; they pick us off one by one." None of this fazes us
because Jesus loves us. I'm absolutely convinced that nothing—nothing living or dead, angelic or demonic, today or
tomorrow, high or low, thinkable or unthinkable—absolutely
nothing can go between us and God's love because of the
way that Jesus our Master has embraced us. (The
Message—Rom 8:35-39)*

The earthly priest makes sacrifice for sin daily, continually from day to day, never ceasing, unending. Jesus Christ
made one single sacrifice (the giving of Himself) for sin, one
final sacrifice, everlasting, all sufficient—the one of perfection, taking care of our sins now and for evermore. Because
of this we can now walk right into the throne room, any
time, without presenting other sacrifices.

There is no need for further sacrifice because this sacrifice was sufficient to take the imperfect person and make him
into a perfect person, in the sight of God. You do not need an
earthly priest anymore—Jesus became our eternal Priest,
opening the curtain so that we can go right into the holy of
holies (the throne room) and talk to God the Father personally. WELL, GLORY TO OUR GOD HALLELUJAH==
PRAISE HIS HOLY NAME!!!!!!!!!!

I have personally found out or come to the conclusion
that there is no way that we can ever say or promote enough
about what Jesus has done for us as individuals. It is so very
awesome that I cannot find words that will completely
describe the fullness included in it.

As David said:
"I saw God before me for all time,
Nothing can shake me; He is right by my side.
I am glad from the inside out; ecstatic;
I have pitched my tent in the land of hope.

I know you will never dump me in Hades;
I will never even smell the stench of death.
You have got my feet on the life-path,
With Your face shining sun-joy all around."!
(The Message—Acts 2:25-28)

Again, the old plan was just a hint of what is included in the new plan—when Jesus said "you don't want sacrifice and offerings", He was talking about the old plan. He set aside the first (old) plan that He might bring the new plan into order by the once for all time sacrifice of Jesus—Who, when He had completed the sacrifice, goes and sits down by the side of God the Father.

Jesus, our Messiah, by passed the old plan, the sacrifices of animals, and instead gave of Himself, the shedding of His own blood, paying the supernal price for freeing you and me, once and for all. Remember that He was sinless perfection, giving Himself for sin and imperfection.

Now, are you getting or do you have the correct picture of Jesus' endeavor for you? We each and everyone need to keep this constantly and forever engraved in our minds and spirit, that it will keep us aware (at all times) of what He has done for us that we might have the privilege and opportunity to be able to approach freely the throne of grace in our lives, walking in His ways of perfection, pleasing Him.

Please notice, that I did not say that this would be easy, and surely I am not saying it at the present—there will be trying and rough times (in the valley)—don't think that we are better than our Master and Saviour, we are His servants, so take the problems that come to you as opportunities to grow by, and your relationship with Him will become sweeter and greater—just praise Him when you have the chance of suffering for Him. Your Father is the umpire (referee) so if you miss the ball on strike three, just keep striking until you hit, you are never out when you are trying to get all of Him in your life.

He is looking for and desiring possessors (these are the people that really know Him, not just know of Him or about Him), this can in no way be stressed enough. When trusting and walking in Him as possessors then you are pleasing Him. James says that faith and works go hand in hand—he says show me your faith without works and I will show you a dead person—also show me your works without faith and I will show you a dead person.

My Father God tells me that His ways are so simple, but man takes them and adds to or subtracts from and they are tripping up over them because of their changes. Just walk in His simplicity—don't listen and be led away by the things man might say or do that is not fully and completely in God's simple ways. Peter says that we are a chosen people, a royal priesthood, a *peculiar* people to show others the night-and-day difference He made for you—you were nothing but now you are everything in Him.

So it is time to roll up your sleeves, so to speak, and let your spirit through the Holy Spirit lead you into the way of life shaped after God's life, being influential, energetic, and literally blazing a way of holiness by the life you are living for Him and through His ability.

His says He wants and needs availability and He will lead you in His ways such as you have never known. He wants you to come into intimate fellowship with Him and then He can be free to pour His blessings out on you.

Your old man or birth came from sperm of man but your new birth comes from the living Word of God that goes on and on forever, never ending—the life that Jesus lived, never doing and saying one thing wrong or amiss—so we are to say or do nothing evil, but to spend our time doing good and running after peace—this will get God's approval. Since Jesus went through everything that we are or will ever be, we need to know how He thinks and what He would do in each situation. We have already given our time to worldly life, now let us put our time and efforts to something that is the most important thing that has ever happened in our lives. We have become dead to the world and its ways, and alive to God and His ways, so let us be true to God in all our ways (without Him we are nothing, but with Him we are every-thing)—let His love flow through us, our lives showing forth the reality of His Word and His presence being upon us and through us continuously—this is the Godly life. Everything that brings about a life that is pleasing God has been mirac-ulously given to us just because we are getting to know Him personally and intimately—this because of the One that made possible the invitation for us to come to God.

The foregoing is a revealing of Jesus, the Messiah, that God gives us, that we might understand more fully all that Jesus went through for us and literally gave of Himself. The God Who Is, The God Who Was, The God Who Is Just Before Coming, gives us, His children, His best—there is no better, because He gives of Himself through His Son, Jesus Christ our Messiah, Who loves us, Who blood-washed us from sin in this life, then making us a kingdom of priests for His Father and our Father God—the Alpha, the Omega, the Beginning, the End, the A to Z.

Consider This

"It won't be long now, He (Jesus, My Son) is on the way,
He will show up most any minute.
But anyone who is right with Me thrives on loyal trust;
If he cuts and runs, I won't be happy."
(The Message—Heb 10:37-38)

How very blessed are the readers of this because they are reading and receiving the Message hot off the press of God. How very blessed are the hearers and keepers of the words of this message, that was given to us from Him. How very, very blessed, are those who receive this message and walk the walk of life with Him before others that they might see God's presence shining forth through you, causing them to become hungry and wanting to receive all God has to give them, too.

This, in essence, is the message that God gave me, at this particular time and situation, so I am being obedient and passing it on to you, that you might be blessed continually and unlimited by Him—the God of Light, that very pure Light, because there is no trace of darkness in Him—never has been, and never will be.

The following words that fits the situation so very well was written by my wife before she went to be with her Heavenly Father:

Come unto Me all you that are laboring and heavy laden.
Come unto Me and I will give you rest.
Lay down your weary head upon My shoulder and come
unto Me My child and you will be blest.
The heavy burdens of each day gets you down. You were
not made to carry the weight of this world.
You were made to worship Me and give Me pleasure.
You are My joy, My love, My crowning jewel.
I made you for Myself, not for another, you are My Bride
and I will carry your load.
I love you with a love that never falters.
Walk with Me, talk with Me along life's road.
I did not make you to have trials of the enemy.
It was not My plan for man to go astray.
I suffered the loss of man's rejection on Calvary so that
now you can walk with Me along life's way.
It is not My desire for you to hurt or be in anguish.
Come unto Me and let Me have (carry) all your care.
Walk in My rest with Me supplying your every need and
there will be no burden you cannot bear.

Fasting and prayer made an entrance into the king's presence for Esther, it gets us into our King's presence. Beauty gets us fleshly attention, the Spirit gets us God's attention.

Faith is the ability to believe what you want exists, even though you cannot presently see it. God will never advance your instructions beyond your ability of obedience.

As a summation of the above Jesus wants to ask you the question "Do you love Me?" Jesus asked Peter the same, "Peter do you love Me more than these?" Peter answered "Yes, Master, You know I love You". Jesus, tells Peter,

"Feed My lambs". The second time Jesus asks Peter, "Simon, do you love Me?" Peter answers, "Yes, Master, You know I love you". Jesus tells him, "Shepherd My sheep". Then the third time Jesus asks, "Simon, do you love Me"? Can't you imagine how upset Peter was getting at this point, so he answers, "Master, you know everything there is to know, so You just have to know that I love You". Jesus then tells Peter to "Feed My sheep—follow Me".

Do you really think that you are honored or respected more than Peter? What is the Lord telling you to be and do at this very point? Surely we are to take up the cross and follow Him wherever, whenever, and however He tells, leads and guides, laying out His ways before us in very instructed terms. Don't you truly love Him enough to be His yielded, open, obedient vessel, that He is looking for—He says He is interested in our availability, then He can and will take that and do and make great and wondrous things happen. Spend much time in praise and worship, going into His throne room, receiving the intimacy that He has and wants to share with each and every one of us, as His children.

* * *

Acknowledgment to Father God

It is with much awe and humbleness that I try to express my appreciation and thankfulness to You, Father God, my El Shaddai. How can I begin to give quality honor to You, Lord? Words seem so very insignificant and incapable of expression that could ever reach You.

I want to thank You for giving and expressing Yourself in so many unlimited ways to get the job done that You want and desire to be accomplished. I am so very aware that Your ways are not my ways, but You will take the obedient vessel and show Yourself in and through it (and I sense that You just enjoy and love doing that so very much).

You literally show Yourself through Your Words that You give and speak to us, so I just ask that in the following pages, as people read them, that Your Presence, Your Glory, will be extolled unlimited in the lives of all. May You bring Your children into praise and worship, the kind of worship that brings You on the scene in reality, into a personal confrontation with You.

This relationship will bring about a close intimacy, which

is the top of the line in the fellowship with Him, then He can give us all the things that He is characteristic of. Through this relationship of intimacy He can and will get done all the things He has been wanting to do and could not because of the unopened channels. He says that the Most Holy Place experience is for everyone of His children. He does not want His children limited in anyway, but the limitation comes through choices made by His children. He made us vessels of choice, whether voluntary or involuntary, and He has to honor each and every one of them (the choices we make). We even have to make a choice to be aware of the choices we are making, whether good or bad. This is the Father God's ways and He wants us to make the right choices so we can be accepted into His unlimited ways of living.

* * *

Journey to the
Most Holy Place

L et us consider now that we are going on a journey to a place that we have never been before. When going on a journey we need to know what to expect as much as we possibly can, but on this trip you will be at a slight disadvantage. Not many have explored this land before, only a few reports of those who have been there, so be ready for the unexpected, at any point of the journey, which is the rule of the day when you explore GOD'S DOMAIN. In 1st Corinthians, the apostle Paul reaches out for those hearts who yearn for the Lord's heart; drawing them from one time to another, giving a quick glimpse into the realm of God's fullness which when experienced it becomes the quest of him who enters.

The people of Corinth were known for their unruly, heavy drinking, and loose, free sex. When Paul arrived with the Message, many of the people became believers in Jesus, but they brought their reputations right on in the church with them. The Corinthians were not much different from most churches today, just muttering around the Holy Place, stumbling over different issues, while excelling in others. This gift realm, that we are arriving at, is a realm of duo; flesh will be there. In the partial light of the Holy Place, a light created only by the candlesticks of the Spirit, he explains how various gifts can be at work in a singular, many membered body. He speaks of prophecy and of tongues and of order, keeping a balance between each truth, keenly aware of the church's carnality and leaning toward legalism, and other things looking for selfish gain. And in all this Paul concludes that this is all too technical by saying, "Let me show you a more excellent way".

Paul begins to unveil the fullness of God within the veil to the confused, hungry, and yet honest brethren.

He tells of the precious divine motivation behind every gift, every ministry and every unction of the Spirit, **"THE LOVE OF GOD".** You will be putting your activities on trial to discern your motivations and your goals.

Paul reminiscences Jesus' conversation while quoting "Many will come to me in that day and say, 'Lord, Lord, did we not prophecy in your name, and in your name cast out demons? Did we not do many mighty works in Your name?' And I will answer them, 'I never knew you; depart from Me, you who practice lawlessness'."

The only pure motivation is genuine relationship with God, this being born and nurtured as the fullness of the new covenant is experienced. The new covenant is experienced where the blood is sprinkled on the mercy seat and the mercy seat is within the veil.

Paul knows that the only real hope for the church, and for you and me, lies within the veil. The outward experiences of the Spirit-filled life has significance only if they are the result of deep inner relationship with Jesus and of a continuous genuine heart change. There is a greater realm of experience and power that is being missed; that of fullness or completeness, which only come through purity and cleanliness.

The gift realm is an experience "along the way", not the full expression of God's heart; so abandon the fleshly realm, the partial, and go on to manhood or fullness. Take the layout of the temple—the outer court corresponds to the conversion experience and gives entry into the Holy Place—the second court, the candlesticks, the oil and the flame correspond to a humanity filled with the Holy Spirit. The outer court experience, while giving you eternal life, is illuminated by natural light—in the Holy Place flesh and spirit work together to produce light—this realm of mixture being the realm of the partial, the child, the imperfect, the dark mirror; while within the veil there is no mixture—it is all **HIM**. Within the veil the work of man is not permitted, the sweat of man has no place—for God alone is pre-eminent, He does all the initiating. The realm within the veil is all **SPIRIT**—what you see you can see by the light of God—no natural sun, no burning candlesticks—it is the unapproachable light of His shining and pulsating from between the cherubin above the mercy seat—in this realm is light and mercy—no warfare, no sickness, no pain. Within the veil is the Perfect, **the Man**, the Fullness—within the veil is the **Lord alone**.

In the realm of the partial, the Holy Place, abides faith and hope—in the Most Holy Place abides **Love**. Faith and hope causes you to look forward to what you have not attained—love is a (now) experience—describing the greatest encounter, the present reality—His love shining in and filling your heart with Himself.

So with your heart crying out for Him it is time to begin the journey. Those who seek Him in all His Glorious Splendor will find Him!!!!!!GLORY, GLORY!!!!!!!

The Lord is saying that there is a place with Him that you have not accessed fully yet, but He so desires and so wants you to. He has always wanted His glory of His Majesty and Presence with His own. You are beginning a journey that you are not familiar with, one that is very thrilling, dangerous, and for sure it will cost you your life as you know it now, because we cannot enter beyond the veil carrying any baggage whatsoever. Beyond this we can stand within the veil without any malice, any haughtiness, or any other of the many things that have kept us from it.

As you become aware of His presence your heart cries, and aches for the nearness, the fellowship, the intimacy, and His love and tenderness, being aware that life holds nothing else for you. And for sure, this is one time that you cannot fake an experience with God. All of man's battles are consumed victoriously here in the ultimate presence of God Almighty; there is nothing from yesterday that can hold on to you. You are standing in the presence of your future—**FATHER GOD ALMIGHTY,** and He is saying "**Come, My son, the Blood of My Son, My Firstborn Son,** has made you clean"**. All at once you become aware of "when we see Him, we will be like Him". You can see all of your doctrines go, also your talents, gifts and ministry has to go for there is no need of these along with personal ambition, greed and lust, bitterness, grudges and whatever else there is. You have lost your urge or push for religious activities as the Lord says to you, *"My son, the Blood of Jesus has been sprinkled to the mercy seat, come hither!"*. At this time a light from above the mercy seat envelopes you and you are clothed with the unapproachable light of God. *"For he who saves his life will lose it, but he who loses his life for My sake will find it. He must increase, but I must decrease"*. You just know that He is changing you into something that will be pleasing to Him. He looks with anguish at the pile of rubbish you have left laying at the mercy seat and with a mighty breath of flames the whole pile is consumed, leaving you with a wonderful, exalted feeling such as you have never known before, being aware that nothing can ever separate you from the love of your Father again. As you sit on the mercy seat you begin to experience and feel the feelings of the Lord as you look at the unregenerated state of even the most zealous believers. Your heart reaches out in pity and sorrow, the Spirit of prayer moans in you, as you realize how little of the Lord most people know and how little of Him most are content to experience. Your vision has taken on yet another realm; you have been drastically, supernaturally changed only to proceed into the next step of being raptured in the Lord.

The church has barely begun to experience and understand what all this means, under estimating His power and ability, which is far more than she has ever dreamed. God is for the here and now, inviting you to dwell with Him in sweetness and fullness of His manifest presence within the veil of the Most Holy Place.

The depth of man's barrenness is greater than you can imagine—the depth of your own barrenness now reaches its full impact—think of being in a place of perfection, and all you see and feel is completeness.

Now you are compelled by the same love and mercy that moved the Lord Jesus to make the ultimate sacrifice. You find yourself before the Father, interceding and ministering on behalf of the needs you see, being totally forgetful about yourself, totally consumed in Him. You ask the Lord fewer and fewer questions as His life increases in you—your own way continues to decrease—you are responding to the Lord, Who is ever-increasing in your life. The manna is not falling from Heaven anymore, for it is welling up within your innermost being. You have taken your place as part of the bread broken so that life may come forth. Your will aligning with His and your spirit submitting to His. Your heart that once beat only for Him is beating with Him, for His church and for those who call upon Him for help. Your desires are becoming His desires, your motivation His motivation, and your joy His joy. <u>Your cry to the church is "come up hither!</u>

come up where He is, where there is no striving, but only flourishing life. Come up hither, where there is no more going out of the camp to gather bread for the day. Come to the place where you become one with this **Eternal Bread,** broken yet glorified for His sake and to fulfill His purposes. Come up hither, where there is no more going out but only flowing". You have entered His rest, His life now freely flows through you, a yielded vessel—you do not make life changes—He does.

You cannot heal the broken-hearted or free the prisoner, only He has the power. You see need, brokenness, heartache, despair, pain, suffering, hopelessness and insecurity teeming in the masses of humanity. You began to think His thoughts, dream His dreams, love with His love, being moved by His emotions, ministering by His power for His purposes. "Your Kingdom come, Your will be done on earth as it is in Heaven." Like His eyes, your eyes now go to and fro over the land as you pray, respond, intercede and minister from within the veil—your life is not your own. You are beginning to discover yet another secret, the secret of spiritual warfare.

Paul found himself in a constant battle with the Christians at Corinth—he would get one problem solved and three more would appear. The authority of God was being bucked through Paul, by this church. It truly took the graces of God to propel Paul in a farther and deeper walk with Him.

Yes, you will have warfare, but it will not be you that are fighting the battles, it will be the Lord because He has become your Avenger.

The following words were given, by the Lord, to my wife:

ARE YOU LISTENING?

Listen to the wind of the Spirit,
Listen to the stirring of the leaves
Listen to the voice of the Father
calling His own unto Him
Listen to the voice of the Gentle Shepherd
calling from the mountains and the shady glenn
The Spirit goes forth into all the world
convicting and convincing the world of sin
Then bringing the wandering ones unto the Saviour,
rescuing them from the lion's den.
Hearken unto the voice of the Spirit,
Let Him be your truth and guide,
He is the one sent by the Father
to be your teacher, helper, and to walk by your side.
Listen to the wind of the Spirit,
Listen to the rustling of the leaves.
There seems to be a stirring in the air,
Shaking people from their beds of ease.
There is a shaking of the branches,
Loosening from all worldly care,
He is bidding and drawing His own unto Him,
It is the same wind as on the day of Pentecost,
The rushing mighty wind of His power,
It is blowing away the dross,
It is blowing the dross away from my people,
And still setting man free this day and hour.
There has never been a time when the Spirit
ceased to be or lost His power,
It is only in the eyes of sinful men,
Trying to destroy His miracle power.
GLORY, HALLELUJAH TO OUR HEAVENLY
FATHER!!!!!!!

* * *

YOUR MOVE

Take into account that great love and achievements involve great risks. When you lose, do not lose the lesson Follow the three r's:

respect for self,
respect for others,
responsibility for all your actions.

Remember that not getting what you want is sometimes a wonderful blessing. Learn the rules; do not let a little dispute injure a great friendship, when you realize you have made a mistake, take immediate steps to correct it. Spend some time alone everyday; open your arms to change, but do not let go of your values in Him. Remember silence is sometimes the best answer. A loving atmosphere in your home is the foundation for your life. Share your knowledge, it is a way to achieve immortality. Remember that the best relationship is one in which your love for each other exceeds your need for each other.

* * *

I would like to list some words of a song:

WHAT A WONDERFUL SAVIOR

I have found a wonderful Savior,
Jesus Christ, the soul's delight!
Every blessing of His favor,
Fills my heart with hope so bright.

Life is growing rich with beauty,
Toil has lost it's weary strain,
Now a halo crowns each duty,

And I sing a glad refrain.

Heavenly wisdom He provides me,
Grace to keep my spirit free,
In His own sweet way He guides me,
When the path I cannot see.
O what splendor, O what glory,
O what matchless power divine,
Is the Christ of the gospel story,
Christ, the Savior Who is mine!

Jesus is the joy of living,
He's the king of life to me,
Unto Him my all I'm giving,
His forevermore to be.

I will do what He commands me,
Anywhere He leads I'll go!
Jesus is the joy of living,
He's the dearest friend I know!
GLORY, GLORY, GLORY, GLORY!!!

* * *

SOMEONE CARES

Once I walked down a lonesome road,
confused was I with a heavy load.
No one even seemed to care
nor had any time with me to share.
Then God sent someone my way,
He witnessed to me that very day!!!
I took Christ Jesus into my heart and like He promised, He
did His part.

I still have plenty of ups and downs
but I will be ready when the trumpet sounds!!
For now my Jesus is really a friend to me.
I walk in His blessed light, and now I can see.
Who is this Christ to me, you say??????
He is my strength and my guide each day.
Jesus came to give us life anew,
so He commissions me to share it with you!!!!!!

* * *

YOUR PURPOSE

Purpose to seek Him
He will be your reward

Purpose to know Him
He will reveal Himself to you

Purpose to follow Him
He will lead the way

Purpose to enjoy Him
He will be your closest friend

Purpose to praise Him
He will be your song

Purpose to trust Him
He will be your provider

Purpose to be totally His
He will be totally yours.

Yes, Jesus is your Rock, your Salvation, your Redeemer.

* * *

The Affection of
Your Heart

Let Jesus show you the affection of your heart!
Don't you just love the way the Lord says things and what He says. Christ is seeking for the soul who will receive His love, and the real Christian who is seeking for Christ will receive His love. Both are practicing the unalterable law of God, "Give and it shall be given unto you". There is a thing that is dearer to God than anything else, it is the same thing that is dear to every man—**that is the affection of your heart.**

Christ is seeking the affection of mankind, the union of man's spirit with His, for without man's affection there can never be that deep union of the Spirit between God and man that makes possible the richness of life, made glorious in His indwelling. That is why the love of God is shown in the Word as the one supreme attraction to draw the soul of man in returned affection. You can give the Lord your money, your property, your brain and all the other things that are usually considered to be excellent; but if you withhold your affections from Him and give them to another, the Word says you are an adulterer. So long as religion exists you will never be able to separate real religion from the emotions of the soul. What will we do and what will we think when we become the habitation of God—what will be the tenderness of our emotions, of our souls, what will be the depth of our feelings, what will be the growth of our capacity to love??

God lives in the spirit of man, the spirit of man reaching out into the boundless, touching the almightiness of God, discerning His nature, approaching His power, securing His almightiness. God lives in a man's flesh, giving off vibrations of God life, God power, God indwelling in his hands, God indwelling in his bones and marrow—a habitation of God.

The Spirit of God is like the bread that the disciples distributed to the multitude, it became filled with the Spirit of God—as they brake more came in its place—the Spirit of God is creative, generative, constructive and the more you give the more you receive. He grows, He magnifies in your soul as you share Him with others.

* * *

The Spirit of God Versus Flesh

No eye has seen, no ear has heard, no mind has conceived what God has prepared for those who love Him, but He will reveal these things to us by His Holy Spirit; for the Holy Spirit searches all things, even the deep things of God. For what man can know the thoughts of a man except by the spirit of a man; in the same way man cannot know the thoughts of God without the Spirit of God.

We speak not the words taught us by human wisdom but words taught by the Holy Spirit, because we have received the Holy Spirit from God, not the spirit of the world. Man without the Holy Spirit does not accept the things that come from God because they are foolishness to him. He cannot understand them because they are Spiritually discerned. We speak of the secret Wisdom of God which was hiddened from the world but is being revealed to us by the Holy Spirit and we understand because we have the mind of Christ. Again, there is a wisdom of the world, and there is a Wisdom of God—the choice is ours because we are vessels of choice—He does not force us, He only enforces the choices that we make, whether good or bad—we determine by choice where we will spend eternity.

* * *

The Wisdom of God

This Wisdom of God was before His works or acts of old, even the creation of the earth. Wisdom was manifested in the plan of God and by Wisdom God made all things—including the mountains and hills, the earth, the fields, and the dust of the earth.

Wisdom was present in the creation of the heavens and the preparing of boundaries, the skies and clouds, and all the orderly depths—including the seas and the land obeying His boundaries.

Wisdom was beside Him in all of His works, as master or director, being daily with Him, His delight and joy, His rejoicing—He rejoiced in delight for the saints, the godly who inhabited the earth of His making.

God's Wisdom says to those who lack understanding, the easily led astray and wavering, to come eat at my table and live. Come walk in the way of understanding and insight. Wisdom brings knowledge and understanding, which is a necessity of the saints.

Wisdom was and is in all of God's creations, so He wants the man that He created in His likeness to be a vessel of His Wisdom, in this present life (yes, particularly and most surely, in this life). Truly there is worldly wisdom and there is Godly wisdom—the choice is ours, what is your choice???

* * *

Speak God's Word

Father, because of Your Word, I have the Spirit of wisdom and knowledge of God. So I covenant with You now to always give voice to Your Word. I will never give voice or place to the words of the enemy. I give place to the Spirit of God for You have given the angels charge over me and my way is the way of the Word. Because Your Word is in me, I am redeemed from the curse of the law and from the powers of darkness. The greater One dwells in me and causes me to prevail. My pathway is health and prosperity because You have redeemed from sickness, disease, cancers, heart problems and poverty.

Galatians 3:13—*(Christ redeemed us from that selfdefeating, cursed, life by absorbing it completely into Himself. Do you remember the scripture that says, "Cursed is everyone who hangs on a tree"? That is what happened when Jesus was nailed to the cross; He became a curse, and at the same time dissolved the curse—(The Message)*—the Word is in my mouth, it is in my bloodstream, flowing to every cell of my body, is forming itself in my body. The Word is becoming flesh for You sent Your Word and healed me—it causes growths to disappear, sickness to flee, arthritis to go.

My bones and joints function properly, all has to go for the Spirit of God is upon me, His Word is within me. I will fear no evil for the Word of the Lord comforts me.

The Lord tells me—I am far from oppression, fear does not come near me, no weapon formed against me shall prosper, but whatever I do will prosper, because I am the redeemed of the Lord and I say so—this is my heritage as the servant of the Lord and my righteousness is of my Father God.

Heavenly Father, I make a covenant with You to voice Your Word. The Spirit of Truth within me will guide me into all truths, will teach me all things, and take of Yours and show it to me. I see these things belong to me, I say they are mine now, the devil shall not steal them from me.

I walk in prosperity, I walk in health, because the Greater One is in me and He will put me over and give me victory, the Word of God has come to me and I will not fail, I will not fear, I will not tremble when tragedy seems near, for Your Word will destroy the enemy's work and will keep him far from my house. I loose the angels and ministering Spirits of God to garrison around my home, family, finances, and to guide me into the wisdom of God.

Father, because my mind is stayed on You, You keep me in perfect peace, I will lift up my hands and rejoice, I will stand to the true height of Your Word and I will not let it out of my sight. I will not enter into the fight because the angels of God are working for me, and the Spirit of God within me will reveal the hidden things to me. I say I have perfect knowledge of every situation, I do not lack for the Wisdom of God for I have the mind of Christ. The Wisdom of God is formed within me, so I rejoice!!! The enemy is defeated, God is exalted, and Your Word is Lord of my life!!!!!

Father, I covenant with You to be what You said I am, even though I do not look like, I may not act like it, or feel like it, but You said I am so I must be. I will come boldly to the Throne of Grace with rejoicing, I will speak what You say, I will walk in Your victory, I will praise Your Name, from this day I will never be the same!!! <u>Thank You and Glory to Your Precious Name—El Shaddai</u>!!!!!!!

Power of Choice

L et us remember that the power to make choice is the greatest power that God gives to man—so put it to use, meditate, encourage and strengthen yourself by using the word at all times. Don't be mere professors but grow into being possessors—think in the spirit by shutting your mind off. If you want kingdom power you must live under kingdom rules.

If you want to know God better ask Him to put you in favor with someone who knows Him better than you do.

If it does not bring you **love, joy, peace and comfort** it does not come from God. As we minister to Jesus He gives us what we need, want, and desire—just know that God will do it for you.

* * *

A Good Prayer to Pray for Our Nation

Almighty Father God Who has given us this nation and good heritage, we do humbly beseech You that We may always prove ourselves a people mindful of Your favor and glad to do Your blessed will.

Lord, defend us in our liberties, and fashion us into one people by uniting the multitudes brought out of many kindreds and tongues.

Save us from violence, discord, and confusion, among ourselves and abroad; from pride and arrogances and from every work or move of the enemy that comes against us in many and various ways.

Bless our land with honorable industry, sound learning and pure manners—let us walk godly before You and live as You desire us to live, that You might do these things that we are asking You to do.

Lord we surely ask that You give Your wisdom to those whom we entrust the responsibility of our government, that we might have peace and justice at home, and that we might be a nation of godly praise, showing forth to the nations of the world.

Help us Lord that our hearts might ever be in a state of thankfulness to You, so that in the day of trouble, we might stand firm and not fail, because of our trust in You. Thank You so very much for Your tender mercies and loving kindnesses that You are continuously bestowing upon us. In the Holy Name of Jesus Our Lord, Amen and Amen!!!!!!!

* * *

Jesus Is Our Miracle Worker

We are to call Jesus our miracle worker—He will give us what we need, want, and desire. We know that God promised it in His word, and when we know that He will do it, thank Him for it and praise His wonderful name.

We learn how to do it by studying His word—as you find it you will learn to have no shame, so that in using His Word, God can send you whatever, whenever, wherever He so desires.

Make the devil obey you—confusion, cancer, diseases, etc., must obey as you speak the word into effect. You are in a spiritual warfare so take the weapons that the Lord gives you and pull down the strongholds of the enemy.

Speak with authority in Jesus name by faith, do not go by feelings—have knowledge in God's word of what is yours:

{1} you have to be delivered from pride and not be ashamed of the gospel of Christ, this takes much prayer.

{2} Don't ever harm another for you reap what you sow, ask God to give you favor with people who know more about Him than you do.

If you don't know the power and authority in Jesus name He will never send you to hard cases. Get free from people, don't ever let your prayers fade out or get weak, let them get stronger—devils don't listen to or obey weak people—as long as you resist the devil he can't get into you. It is all in Jesus name with authority—never lose your peace when casting out devils.

Laying on of hands is a New Testament doctrine and you are obligated to obey it.

You cannot get the work of God done through unbelief or ignorance. Don't ever change no matter what the devil does—don't get nervous, stay steadfast and don't wear yourself out. Always learn to build up and not tear down. The devil will put you to a test sometimes to see if you will give up—if you don't he has to go. If you lack wisdom, ask God for it. Pray before ministering to anybody—you will always need God's wisdom, always, ask for wisdom and believe you have it before you see it.

* * *

Food for Thought

The New Testament is contained in the Old Testament
The Old Testament is explained in the New Testament
The New Testament is concealed in the Old Testament
The Old Testament is revealed in the New Testament
The New Testament authenticates the Old Testament
The Old Testament anticipates the New Testament
The New Testament lies hidden in the Old Testament
The Old Testament lies open in the New Testament
The Old Testament predicts a person
The New Testament presents that person

Mat 6:33-34 tells us *to give our entire attention to what God is doing right now, and don't get worked up about what may or may not happen tomorrow. God will help you deal with whatever hard things come up when the time comes. (The Message).*

* * *

Listen to the Mind of God

Do you know that the sins of violence or vileness in men's lives or ways of living originates in the mind? He is the character of what he thinks—if he thinks evil he will be evil, if he thinks good or holy he will be good or holy. In other words, it is what comes out of the heart of man, so we need to keep our minds on the Blessed Trinity. Man can and does receive into his nature the Spirit and power of the living God, which can and does drive out every sensuous thought, when you ask and allow it.

This same Heavenly Power in us dissolves diseases and restores bodies to normal. When disease germs appear on our bodies it makes us feel ugly and unclean, so we must speak His Word over all things that are unclean, removing them from our very being. The Lord wants us to use this Holy Power to cleanse ourselves and others.

Our lives are to be satisfactory lives flowing from and through Him—showing Him wherever, whenever, however He so desires and needs us to be.

* * *

The following caption is one recording of many that was given by the Lord to my wife (Bobbie Coates), over a period of time. You can find all the other recordings listed in the book, "**Come Away My Beloved**", compiled by Leon Coates, in obedience to His Heavenly Father's request. Each and every one of them are very anointed. If you cannot find this book at your local bookstores please get in touch with me at the address on the back cover of this book you are reading or on the first pages.

How to Obtain God's Light and Love

God says, let the love light that you see shining out of My eyes flow into your very being. It is My love, My light, that penetrates the darkness—the dark recesses of your soul—the depths of your very being—the light dispels the darkness. Take time to look into My eyes of love and become what I am—that is love. All the cares of the world will roll away when you live in the realm of My love.

Deep calls unto deep—My Spirit within you is calling you into this love. Don't get your eyes on love—get your eyes on Me—I am the one who imparts love. You never get love by trying, only by being—looking unto Me and at Me and being in My presence.

Come unto Me for what you need—My Word tells you what you should be but you can never attain it. It only comes by looking unto Me—if you could have done it there would have been no purpose of My dying—no purpose in My fulfilling the law. As you come to Me and commit your all to Me and ask for the things you need, you are walking in the Spirit. When you do it yourself, you are living under the law. Walking in the Spirit takes practice just as a little child taking their first steps—they fall, cry, and get hurt many times by just trying, so it is with the Spirit. Learning to walk in the Spirit is not always pleasant—there are rough, hilly, places and terrains but there comes a place that is level ground as far as the Spirit is concerned and you walk every step in My righteousness. Don't fret about learning to walk—only fret if you are not learning, for then you are stagnated, doing nothing.

The lessons you are learning are hard but valuable—you are learning hardness as a soldier—you are learning you can stand even when the battle is hot and raging—you are learning you don't fall just because war is waged against you, so stand fast, unmovable, in the place I have put you—you have not failed—you are not going under. Just keep your eyes on Me and I will bring you through, just like Peter when he kept his eyes on Me, he walked on the water and through the storm. The storm is raging but continue to keep your eyes on Me and I will bring you through it unharmed.

But you must rely on Me for the enemy is seeking whom he may devour and he will devour you if you get your eyes off Me. He knows as long as you are looking only to Me he is defeated—he also knows when you get off your faith and into the flesh. Be vigilant and watch—you are worried about so many things and only one is necessary, like I told Martha, the one needful thing is sitting at My feet and learning of Me. Continue to seek Me and put Me first place and I will take care of the adversary.

The word that is hid in your heart is word that cannot be taken away from you—the more you hide in your heart the more is manifested in your body (surroundings). It is only the hidden man of the heart that really counts—he is the one that is really manifested and if you are feeding him My Words, My thoughts, My actions, he will respond by feeding them back to you as you need them. If you feed him full of negatives, that is what you will receive back, only what you feed him will be given back.

The hard knocks and the heavy loads are produced by wrong feeding. All you will ever get back from your inner man is what you put in. Store up treasures of My Word in your heart and treasures will be available to you when you need them.

Fret not at others inconsistencies and short comings but continue to store up treasures in your heart. Take every opportunity to store up these treasures and then rejoice— rejoice in Me always. Never let others get you down—if you come down to their level you will not have anything to pour out. But keep filling up the jar—keep filling up the vessel and the good things you put in will flow back out of you to others and you will become a blessing.

Scorners should be ignored—don't even take the time to entertain their words—spend no time on their thoughts. Just spend time in My Word storing up treasures and the treasures you store up will be a supply for many).

* * *

Sowing of God's Seed

In my relationship with my Father, He is telling me that the specific instructions of His plan to us cannot be complete without me spending some time talking and telling you about the planting or sowing of seed.

The formerly listed information on the New and Old Testaments will surely be included and involved in the seed situation—so grab hold and let us get started.

In the beginning was the Word—*the Word was first, the Word present to God, God present to the Word, the Word was God, in readiness for God from day one. The Word became flesh and blood, and moved into the neighborhood—we saw the glory with our own eyes, the one-of-a-kind glory, like Father, like Son—generous inside and out, true from start to finish. (The Message).*

Everything was created through Him; nothing—not one thing!!—came into being without Him. What came into existence was Life, and that Life was Light to live by. The Life-Light blazed out of the darkness; the darkness couldn't put it out.

So the seed was the Word of God—the seed was God—and the seed was with God—His Word is His seed supply to us—the Holy Bible is a God-seed inventory for us, given to us to live and profit by. No people has ever been quite so blest as we are—everything we need is in the spirit realm, His seed realm.

God said—I am Alpha and Omega—the First and the Last—the Beginning and the End. It is no wonder, then, that the middle chapter of the Bible is the shortest chapter in the Bible—*Psalm 117—Praise God, everybody applaud God, all people! His love has taken over our lives; God's faithful ways are eternal, Hallelujah*!!!(*The Message*) To Him there is no middle ground—He starts and He finishes—He does not stop halfway—He plants, continues to work for the harvest, then gathers—He wants to do this through His vessels (you and me).

I was meditating on seed and planting and God says to me—*without seed there would not be anything.* In the beginning God seeded (spoke) everything that came into existence, into being—seed gives forth new life. Since God has seeded (spoke) everything into being, we **see** that seed gives forth new life. Satan planted his seed and caused the fall of angels, the fall of man—bringing with it seeds of fear, doubt, unbelief, distrust, rebellion, rejection, lusts, resentment, and unforgiveness, just to mention a few of many. Do you know that the devil hates you? Why sow seeds for him to have a harvest? So because of this there arose the need for God to do some more planting or seeding.

It took forty-two generations from Abraham to Christ besides the many generations from Adam to Abraham, to receive the harvest from the seed He planted to bring or fulfill the redemption of fallen man, through Jesus. Don't ever get impatient in the sowing of seed because it takes time for a seed to germinate and spring forth, then comes the cultivating and watering to carry it out to harvest. Jesus was seed planted for you and me—God seed planted all things for you and me—we have new life in Jesus because we have become seed of His Seed—we have the seed of God in us. As we plant this seed that is in us, it will give forth or produce more seed or new life of the same likeness or kind. What kind of seed are you planting?

All people either are or have been guilty of following traditions, doctrines, creeds, denomination, human philosophies, etc.—everyone of these are hand-me-downs. God gives to you first-hand, as His child, the things that He has prepared for us—so let's receive everything He is giving us—not what man tells you.

You see, man is a three-fold being; he is spirit—soul—body. The soul, the emotional, the mental, the will, mainly feeds on anticipation, excitement, enthusiasm, and expectation. Man sows seed through the natural he sees, he hears, he tastes, he smells, he feels, he knows, he understands natural ways. He readily accepts the natural; his faith is in the natural. When he purchases a product he expects and believes that the product is to perform as described by the manufacturer—natural man cannot know what Jesus says because he is not spiritually changed or new; yet he is continually sowing seed of his kind and these seeds produce more of the same.

The Spirit man feeds upon the Bible, the Word, the Seed of God, for instructions and directions, the Holy Spirit being his guide. Jesus gives knowledge to the Spirit man (the new man)—He gives him His mind, His Word, His Seeds. Jesus' Words—Seeds—never fails, never a crop failure, never a defective crop.

When Jesus spoke to the fig tree, His Word, His Seed, was applied and immediately went to work. As soon as it went throughout the entire plant it died. Why is it so hard for us to accept what Jesus says as the truth, the whole truth, and nothing but the truth?

The Product-Word-Seed of Jesus is more super than all natural products-seed with their warrantees, guarantees, etc.

Follow His instructions, directions, and there will never be any product failure.

Man in his natural state is incapable of understanding spiritual things—in fact, spiritual things seem foolish to him. Only those who have developed their spiritual senses are capable of understanding mature things. Spiritual people are not destroyers but restorers of those who have fallen—all being part of the many and various membered body of Christ with God.

Again, there are ninety-six fifteen minute sequences in a twenty-four hour day—how many of these are you giving of yourself to the Lord??? People do a lot of things without even thinking, or putting thought to it before you do it—this has your attention rather than the Lord. You see, we are to take each and everyday, and present it to Him, asking Him to lead and guide us—this means giving Him the things in our ordinary life, which includes eating, sleeping, going to work, even our walking around, and all other things, as an offering, that He might position us where He wants us, when He wants us, how He wants us. I am speaking to you from a gratitude for everything that God my Father has done for me. I can personally tell you, when you take your own hands off of your life and give it all into His hands, you will start experiencing life such as you did not know existed.

"OUR FATHER IS LOVE SO JUST LOVE HIM NOW AND FOREVER MORE—HALLELUJAH!!!!"

"Is there anyone around who can explain God?
Anyone smart enough to tell Him what to do?
Anyone who has done Him such a huge favor
That God has to ask his advice?
Always glory!! Always praise!!
Yes—Yes—Yes
(The Message—Rom 11:34-35)

But, please don't get impatient—first comes the planting of the seed—next comes the travail—then comes the birth!!!!!!!!!!HALLELUJAH!!!!!!!!!!!!!

Seed a thought—reap an act
Seed an act—reap a habit
Seed a habit—reap a character
Seed a character—reap a destiny

* * *

My Father is also saying to tell you that you cannot do
these things without the following,
<u>this tells us what faith is and means</u>...

FAITH

Now faith is the substance (the title deed) of things hoped for, your title deed to eternal life. A title deed is evidence of real estate, so your faith is evidence of your eternal estate in God—(*Heb 11:1—The fundamental fact of existence is that this trust in God, this faith, is the firm foundation under everything that makes life worth living. It is our handle on what we cannot see. The act of faith is what distinguished our ancestors, set them above the crowd—2 Cor 4:18—There is far more here than meets the eye. The things we see now are here today, gone tomorrow, but the things we cannot see now will last forever. The Message).*

1. Faith is taking God at His Word and asking no questions—Heb 11:6

2. Faith is knowing that; "*All things work together for good to them that love God*"—Rom 8:28. Faith does not believe that all things are good, or that all things work well. Faith does believe that all things (good or bad) work together for good to them that love God.

3. Faith has two sides, one side has to do with the intellect. It is an intellectual conviction that Jesus Christ is Lord of lords. The other side has to do with the will, it is a volitional surrender of the will to Jesus Christ as Master—this being seen when Thomas believed and confessed, "My Lord and my God"—Jn 20:28. "My Lord" is or was the volitional surrender; "My God" was intellectual conviction. Together you have saving faith—*(Jn 20:31—These are written down so you will believe that Jesus is the Messiah, the Son of God, and in the act of believing, have real and eternal life in the way He personally revealed it. The Message).* Saving faith is an intellectual conviction that Jesus is God, and a volitional surrender to Him as Lord (Master) of your life—so by faith the mind trusts in God; the heart responds to the love of God; the will submits to the commands of God; and the life obeys the service of God.

4. Faith goes beyond reason because it believes without understanding "why", and it sings in prison—*(Along about midnight, Paul and Silas were at prayer and singing a robust hymn to God. Acts16:25; The Message*—it glorifies in tribulations, *(There's more to come: We continue to shout our praise even when we're hemmed in with troubles, because we know how troubles can develop passionate patience in us, and how that patience in turn forges the tempered steel of virtue, keeping us alert for whatever God will do next—Rom 5:3—The Message)*—it chooses to suffer, *(Choosing rather to suffer affliction with the people of God, than to enjoy the pleasures of sin for a season—Heb 11:25—KJV)*—it accepts all things as part of God's will, *(I want to report to you, friends, that my imprisonment here has had the opposite of its intended effect. Instead of being squelched, the Message has actually prospered—Phil 1:12—The Message).*

You were not born with faith, it comes by hearing the Word of God—Rom 10:17. This is why we are commanded to preach the gospel to every creature so that they might hear and believe—*For whosoever shall call upon the name of the Lord shall be saved. How then shall they call upon Him in whom they have not believed? And how shall they believe in Him of whom they have not heard? And how shall they hear without a preacher? Rom 10:13-14—KJV)*

Now let us look at the armor that comes through faith—you are told to put on the whole armor of God because the Christian life is a warfare, a spiritual conflict. When Paul names all the different parts of the armor, he names the shield and emphasizes its great importance by saying, "above all, take the shield of faith—with this shield of faith nothing can hurt you because you are more than a conqueror through Him.

1. You cannot be saved without faith—Jn 3:36.
2. You cannot live a life of victory over the world without faith—1 Jn 5:4.
3. You cannot please God without faith—Heb 11:6.
4. You cannot even pray without faith—Jas 1:6.
5. You cannot have peace with God without faith—Rom 5:1.
6. You cannot have joy without faith—1 Pet 1:8.
7. You are justified by faith and not by works—Gal 2:16.
8. You are to live by faith—Gal 2:20.
9. You are made righteous by faith—Rom 10:1-4.
10. Christ dwells in your heart by faith—Eph 3:17.
11. You receive the Holy Spirit by faith—Gal 3:2.
12. Whatsoever is not of faith is sin—Rom 14:23.

Do you have "little faith"? Consider Peter up to Pentecost and then consider him afterward. When Jesus came walking on the water in the midst of the storm, Peter asked Jesus that he might come to Him—Jesus said "Come".

1. Peter did the impossible thing of walking on the water

by faith.

2. Then Peter did the conceivable thing—as he saw the storm he took thought and doubted, for a moment loosing sight of Jesus, probably turning back toward the boat.

3. Now Peter does the natural thing by fearing destruction—doubt always breeds fear.

4. Next Peter does the expected thing, he begins to sink—failure.

5. Thank God Peter does the right thing by calling out to Jesus "Lord save me". Jesus immediately reached forth His hand because of Peter's faith and caught him.

6. Peter's faith caused him to walk on water to the boat.

You need a faith that is bigger than the elements that would drag you down to defeat—you can have this kind of faith by prayer and fasting—by feeding your faith on the Word of God you can have mountain moving faith. To have this kind of faith not only requires the above but also demands full intimacy with God the Father. When you go to Him in intimacy and spend much time with Him, then you will see your life take on the Power of God and the Wisdom of God, such as you have never known or seen before—**this is His way.** Don't you just love Him????

Faith is a most important part of a person's living and
walking with Father God:
Faith is when the Word of God is all you need
Faith says what the Word says
Faith is not seen
Faith will wait
Faith has nothing to do with time or feeling or circum-
stances
I have what I ask for because God says so—Mk 11:24
Believe you have the answer when you pray—Mk 11:24;
1 Jn 5:14-15
Faith is the same as the answer

Faith confesses what God says
Hope is the object of what you believe for
Faith never questions
Faith endures—Hope gives up
Faith is just believing, that simply
God's promise and your faith is a valid contract;
Faith thanks and praises God from the heart for the answer
whether it is manifested or not.

Make God your source of supply
Make God's Word final authority in your life

Faith is simply believing and acting on what God says.
When fear knocks let faith answer the door.
You can have all kinds of needs but if you do not have the
faith you will still have the needs.
Attack every problem you have, in faith, in its most
vulnerable spot.
It is what comes from the heart that defiles the body. It is
what we meditate on and put in the heart that comes out to
either defile us or make us alive and holy.
The spiritual unseen must control the physical unseen
and seen.
Winners decide that everything in life I do is profitable,
there is nothing that I have to do (you don't have to do any
works, just freely give of yourself to the Lord, and He will
do the works that He desires through you). We do not
know we have been in prison until we have broken out.
!!!!PRAISE GOD FOR BEING OUR FREEDOM!!!!

Positive self-control is the attitude that you take in being
responsible for causing your own affects in life.
Positive self-expectancy includes: enthusiasm,
optimism and winning. Self-expectancy is number one step
toward winning.

In the spiritual realm there are two worlds or kingdoms—
God and satan.
Positive pressures eliminates negative pressures.
Faith is your victory—faith brings God into the now.

We can say the summation of faith is conviction or persuasion, being coupled with works bringing corresponding
action. James says that they both must be in force for it to be
a reality—he says show me your works (corresponding
action) without faith (conviction or persuasion) and I will
show you death or a corpse—and show me your faith (conviction or persuasion) without your works (corresponding
action) and I will show you death or a corpse. Faith does not
come from religion or church—bible faith is receiving and
doing that which our Father tells us do, faith expresses itself
in works. Dear ones, try this; separate your body and your
spirit and you become a corpse—separate faith and works
and you get the same thing, a corpse or something dead.
There is so much more that can be said concerning faith and
works, but this sums it up rather accurately.

You are of God little children and have overcome
because greater is He who is in you than he that is in the
world. I can do all things through Christ who strengthens
me—so let us who want everything God has for us stay
focused on that goal. If any of you have something else in
mind, something less than total commitment, God will clear
your blurred vision—you will see it yet! Now that we are on
the right track, let's stay on it.

**THANK YOU, FATHER GOD, FOR YOUR LOVING
KINDNESSES AND TENDER MERCIES, TOWARD
US AT ALL TIMES!!!!!!!!!!!!!!!!!!!!**

* * *

Sometime ago the Lord speaks to me as follows:

Leon, you have been taught all your life to have faith in God, haven't you—my answer being, yes sir, I have. He then tells me that He wants me to have the faith **of** God—as I received and accepted this, He brings experience after experience to show forth and materialize the reality of this in my life. There is quite a profound difference in the having faith in God in comparison to having the faith **of** God—you can have faith in God and not really bring about the materialization of it but if you have the faith **of** God you cannot just remain idle in Him—you have to move with Him when He says move and how He determines for you to move, because faith **of** God is a very real part of Him, while faith in God is about Him.

Then later on, as He takes me through the journey to the Most Holy Place, and upon the completion of this, He tells me; I gave you faith **in** God then moved you on to the place where I gave you faith **of** God, now I am giving you faith **with** God. I am at loss of words to explain to you just what all is involved in this step or transaction, except to say that there is truly nothing on this earth that can come close to comparing with this experience. As you think His thoughts and walk His walk, you see Him doing things that you have not seen before—you become aware of a closeness that you have not sensed before—you see things happening right before your very eyes. Your life is a walk of amazement—you are an open, obedient vessel that you see Him working and walking through.

He tells you that all He needs is a yielded, obedient, open vessel, and He will continue showing Himself through this vessel, unlimited and yes I mean unlimited—miracles become (so it seems) common place because He is doing and not you or me. He says that this is the place that He wants all His children to be operating in, because each and every one of His children are members of the body. There are various and many parts in the making up of a body—eyes, nose, ears, teeth, hair, fingers, toes, legs, just to name a few—and each of these parts have to do their part for the body to function properly, so it is with the body of Christ. The Father is saying that all that has been mentioned here is for every member (part) of His body—He wants every child of His to walk in His power and Wisdom, being open, yielded, and obedient to Him, so that He can be seen through them. Our mission in this life is for Him to be seen in us, not us being seen. We must decrease so He can increase.

What a wonderful, glorious, loving Father we serve!!!!!

Don't you just love this kind of Father God that gives Himself to us in this active and loving faith—the walk of life that He is so pleased with, to the place that He can say to you at times, "you were obedient to me". Your closeness with Him will grow and your determination to please Him will explode in you—your desire in this life will truly intensify causing you to be single-minded in your destination and purpose on earth. Your one purpose in life will become pleasing Him—wanting to hear Him say "well done, good and faithful one" or "you have been obedient to me". I can truly tell you that receiving such words or comments from Him is surely worth it all, you wonder why your past life was not spent pleasing Him to this point.

Everything is already yours as a gift from God—the world, life, the present, the future, just to mention a very few—because you are in union with **Christ (Who gave you all things), Who is in union with God.**

Don't you know and realize that you are the temple of God—God's house, with Him being the architect and carpenter, Who made you thus. He did not use cheap or inferior materials, but made you to His inspection—so please remember that you are His and that God's temple is sacred (that's you, your body). Everything that you are at the present and everything that you will ever be in the future is because He gave it to you, not because of your works, but because of His love. He is not interested in any of your capabilities, just your availabilities—when we become available, then and only then, can He show Himself in and through us in His power and glory.

We do not rely on the world and the ways of the world, but we rely and learn the ways of God as He leads and teaches us. The world's wisdom does not know our God's Wisdom—the path to God's Wisdom is to be a "fool for God." This truly includes the thought realm—we have to subject the thought area to warfare and bring it into submission. We are what we think about, we will become what we spend our time thinking on. This again is ours in the choice realm.

Yet I have to say, if I have faith to say to the mountain "jump" and it jumps, but I don't have and show forth love, then I am nothing—I can give everything I own and even my life, but if I don't love, I will have gotten nowhere, so without love I am bankrupt, nothing.

LOVE never gives up, love cares more for others than for self, does not want what it does not have, will not strut or have a swelled head, does not forced itself on others, does not have to be first, does not fly off the handle, or keep score of the sins of others, does not revel when given the opportunity, puts up with anything, but takes pleasure in the budding and flowering of truth, always trusts God, and always looks for the best, never looking back but keeps going straight ahead right on into eternity because love never dies.

Right now we have three things to lead us forward to the final completion: Our trust in God, unswerving hope, and extravagant love, with love being the best of the three—our God is LOVE.

Our Heavenly Father has to have love from us because

He is LOVE and will accept nothing short of His love. His love is quite different from the so called love being seen in this world, which surely includes the fleshly love (phileo) with all its toils and snares, but His love is an (agape), a God-love, that He gives and instills in each of His children. He wants this love to be exemplified in and through each and everyone of us as His temples that He can and will flow through.

Let us know that when we cast ourselves completely in His care and Presence, we do not fear anything day or night, no sickness or disease, no harm of any kind because God is our refuge, (He is our Avenger), giving us long life, He keeps His angels guarding and caring for us so that we will not stumble or fall. He teaches us to live well and wisely even in this world and amid the snares and chaos that is all around us (and many times closes in on us trying to trip us up and make us fall, but remain in Him and no defective life or failure can overtake you). Yes, you will become aware that "you can't lose for winning"—that is **the way of our Father God**. He is a giver of _abundant_ life—not a destroyer.

Be prepared, you are up against far more than you can handle on your own. Use every weapon God has issued, so that when it is all over except the shouting, you will be standing on your feet. Learn how to apply truth, righteousness, faith, peace, joy, salvation and power, and all others, because you will need them throughout your life. May we get down on our knees before this awesome, magnificent Father who reaches down from heaven and covers all earth—ask Him to strengthen us by His Spirit, with His glorious inner strength—causing Christ to live in you firmly in love, giving us a life of freedom to walk and live in Him—use this freedom to love one another, to serve one another, that is how this freedom grows. We are motivated and animated by God's Spirit, giving us all the love that we need to accomplish all that He wants us to do. **(this is His way)**

Are you seed-planting and producing like-kind for God to accept and be very pleased with? You will not remain barren, but you will birth God-seed plants or you will birth plants for satan, yet the choice is yours. I know your choice is for God because He gives life and that more abundantly.

Could I pass on some very interesting words that my Father sent my way? Words that Jesus is saying to you and me:

HE IS HUNGERING AND THIRSTING FOR YOU

I stand at the door of your heart, I stand there day and night, even when you are not listening, even when you doubt it is Me. I await even the smallest sign of response, the least whisper of invitation that will allow Me to come in. Whenever you invite Me in, I do come in, always, silent and unseen, so many times, but with infinite power and love and gifts of the Spirit—I come with mercy wanting to forgive and heal, and with love for you beyond your dreams—a love such as I have received from My Father (*I love you the way My Father has loved me, so make yourself at home in My love—Jn 15:10*). I come longing to console you, give you strength, to lift up and bind all your wounds. I bring My light to dispel your darkness and all your doubts.

I come with My power that I might carry you and all your burdens with My grace, wanting to touch your heart and transform your life, filling it with My peace. I know you through and through, everything about you, the very hairs of your head I have numbered, so you see nothing in your life is unimportant to me.

I have loved you and followed you all the years of your life and know your wanderings and problems, your needs and worries, and yes, all your sins—but I tell you again that

I love you, not for what you have or haven't done, but for the beauty and dignity My Father gave you when He created you in His own image.

I love you as you are, I shed My blood for you to win you over to Me. Ask Me with faith, I know what is in your heart, your loneliness, your hurts, rejections, judgments, humiliations—I carried them all before you did.

I know your need for love, your thirsting to be loved and cherished—how often have you thirsted in vain by seeking for love in the wrong places—(*If anyone thirsts, let him come to Me and drink, rivers of living waters will brim and spill out of the depths of anyone who believes in Me this way—Jn 7:37—The Message*)—I cherish you more than you can imagine, to the point of dying on the cross for you.

I thirst, I hunger For You—I thirst to love you, to be loved by you—come to Me and I will fill your heart and heal your wounds, make you a new creation, give you peace, but you must never doubt My mercy, My acceptance of you, My desire to forgive you, My longing to bless you and live My life in you. Open to Me, come to Me, thirst for Me, give Me your life, let Me show you how important you are to Me.

Rev 21:6—*And He further said to me, It is done!! I am the Alpha and the Omega, the Beginning and the End. To the thirsty I (Myself) will give water without price from the fountain (springs) of the water of Life*—Amplified Version—Isa 55:1—*Everyone who is thirsty, come to the waters; and he who has no money, come, buy and eat! Yes, come, buy (priceless, spiritual) wine and milk without money and without the price (simply for the self-surrender that accepts the blessing).*

Trust in Me and everyday ask Me to take charge of your life, and I will promise you before My Father in heaven that I will do miracles as you open to Me, because I thirst for you.

Remember, you are a pilgrim in this life on your journey home—sin cannot satisfy, does not bring you peace, only leaves you more empty—so do not run from Me when you fall but run to Me, giving Me your sins and letting Me be the joy of your Salvation.

There is nothing that I cannot forgive or heal, so come now and unburden your soul—there is one thing that will never change—I thirst, I huunger for you, I stand at your hearts door knocking and wanting to be asked in. Do you find this so hard to believe? Just look at the cross and what I endured for you—have you not yet understood My cross and what was involved there? Listen again to the words I spoke, they will tell you clearly why I endured all this for you; (*I thirst, I hunger—Jn 19:28*). Yes, I thirst and hunger for you—(*in vain I look for one friendly face—not one shoulder to cry on could I find Ps 69:20—The Message*)— all My life I have been looking for your love, I have never stopped seeking to love you and wanting you to love Me. You have tried many things in search of happiness, now try opening your heart to Me, right now, more than you ever have before. As you open the door of your heart and come close enough you will hear Me say to you again and again, not in mere human words, but in the spirit; "No matter what you have done, I love you for your own sake—come unto Me with all your misery and sins, your troubles and needs, and with all your longing to be loved because I stand at the door of your heart and knock—Open to Me, for *I thirst for you.* **"Father God, thank You so very much for Your continued persistence in loving us irregardless of who and what we are."**

* * *

Giving of Yourself

Everyone longs to give himself completely to someone;
To be loved thoroughly and exclusively
But God, to a Christian says
"No, not until you are satisfied, fulfilled, and content with
being loved by Me alone;
By giving yourself totally and unreservedly to Me.
When you discover that only in Me is your satisfaction to
be found, will you be capable of the human relationship
that I have planned for you.
You will never be united with another until you are united
with Me, exclusive of anyone or anything else, of any other
longings or desires.
I want you to stop wishing and planning and allow Me to
give you the most thrilling plan in existence, one that you
cannot imagine—I want you to have the best, please allow
Me to bring it to you.
Just keep watching Me, keep experiencing the satisfaction
that I give, expecting the greatest, keep listening and learning the things I tell you;
Don't be anxious, don't worry, don't look at things you
think you want, that others have—just keep looking up to

Me or you will miss what I want you to see—then when
ready I will surprise you with a love far
more wonderful than anything you have ever dreamed of.
You see, until you are ready and until the one I have prepared for you is ready—until you are both ready and satisfied completely with Me and the life I prepared for you,
you will not be able to experience and accept the perfect
love that exemplifies your relationship with Me.
I want you to have this most wonderful love, dear one, My
chosen one, I want you to see in the flesh the picture I am
giving you of your relationship with Me—enjoying
concretely and materially the everlasting union of the
beauty and perfection and love that I am offering
you with Me.
Know that I love you so supremely and utterly—I am God,
believe it and be satisfied."

This is the same Jesus that hung and died on the cross for
you and me. Dear one, He is alive and well, calling us constantly and continually to Him, with His hands ever
extended toward us, so tenderly, mercifully, and lovingly. As
He gave His life for me, I heard the Holy Spirit wooing and
saying in such a soft, sweet voice, in a whisper—Little
child, lift up your head, Jesus is not dead, He is your victory
flowing down to you ever so plentiful and loving—yes,
Jesus has come back from the grave shouting **His victory
song.** HE IS ALIVE!!!!!!!!!!!GLORY!!!!!!!!!!!!!!!!
HE IS ALIVE!!! NOW
AND FOREVERMORE!!! GLORY!!! HALLELUJAH!!!
PRAISE HIS NAME!!!

* * *

Such a Great Cloud
of Witnesses

Heb. 12:1—(Since we have such a huge crowd of men of faith watching us from the grandstands, let us strip off anything that slows us down or holds us back, and especially those sins that wrap themselves so tightly around our feet and trip us up; and let us run with patience the particular race that God has set before us).

This "great cloud of witnesses" is composed of the people that are listed and described in the former chapter, chapter 11 of Hebrews. You could say that they were pioneers cutting out a trail for us to follow. We can look at them as our faithful, victorious witnesses, who can be a constant encouragement to us. We can see them as veterans who are very wholeheartedly cheering us on through this time of testing and trials, in our earthly lifespan.

We do not struggle alone, neither are we the first to struggle with trials, problems, testing of all kinds, that we face here and now. We must know that others have run this race and very successfully—they were winners, and their witness is to stir us up to run and win also.

The Lord is so awesome and good to us. He did not tell us this life would be easy—in fact He says it would be full of trials and temptations, but He would be with us each step of the way, leading and holding us up to finish the race victoriously and with high honors.

We are required to give up any and everything that would endanger our relationship with God—so we can run with patience against sin, with the power of the Holy Spirit engulfing and controlling us all the way.

We are to keep our eyes upon Jesus (only), running the race, of this course of life, with patient endurance and steadfast persistence. We will most certainly stumble if we take our eyes off Jesus, and start to looking at ourselves or at the circumstances all around us. Anyway, who are we running the race for???—Jesus only, not ourselves, not others—so we must keep our sight on Him. He is the head of all the long train of faith heroes—just as He is the Author and Perfector of our faith. We must observe and consider every part of His life, His sufferings, His victories, and be a follower of Him. We will surely find that running the race and being a victor will be worth all that we put in it and far more than we can ever think or realize in our minds.

Let us ask God the question—who and what are man and woman that You would take a second look at? But yet You made them and put them in charge of Your whole or entire world that You had put into existence, nothing being left out or excluded. Then when man and woman sinned, God still loved them enough to send His only Son to earth in human form to give of Himself, even unto death for you and me, that we might have a means of forgiveness for all our wrong doings. He loved us so much that He wanted us to live with Him forever and still does. He keeps us going now by completing the work of salvation, through Jesus His Son, who was our perfect sacrifice through suffering, that He might lead us to glory.

That is why He can say to His Son:
>"You are God, and on the throne for good,
>Your rule makes everything right.
>You love it when things are right,
>You hate it when things are wrong.
>That is why God, Your God,
>Poured fragrant oil on Your head,
>Marking You out as king,
>Far above Your dear companions."

And again He says to the Son:
>"You, Master, started it all, laid earth's foundations,
>Then crafted the stars in the sky,
>Earth and sky will wear out, but not You.
>They become threadbare like an old coat,
>You will fold them up like a worn-out cloak,
>And lay them away on the shelf.
>But you will stay the same, year after year;
>You will never fade, You will never wear out."

Also:
>"Sit alongside Me here on My throne
>Until I make Your enemies a stool for Your feet."
>(The Message—Heb 1:7-13)

The Holy Spirit says:
>"Today, please listen;
>Don't turn a deaf ear as in 'the bitter uprising,'
>That time of wilderness testing!
>Even though they watched Me at work for forty years,
>Your ancestors refused to let Me do it My way,
>Over and over they tried My patience.
>And I was provoked, oh, so provoked!
>I said, 'They will never keep their minds on God;
>They refuse to walk down My road.'

Exasperated, I vowed,
'They will never get where they are going,
Never be able to sit down and rest.'"
"Today, please listen
Don't turn a deaf ear as in the bitter uprising."
(The Message—Heb 3:7-10,15)

Then God says:
"This time I am writing out the plan in them,
Carving it on the lining of their hearts.
I will be their God, they will be My people.
They won't go to school to learn about Me,
Or buy a book called *God in Five Easy Lessons.*
They will all get to know Me firsthand,
The little and the big, the small and the great.
They will get to know Me by being kindly forgiven,
With the slate of their sins forever wiped clean."
(The Message—Heb 8:10-12)

GLORY HALLELUJAH TO THE FATHER, SON AND HOLY SPIRIT!!!!

* * *

All the way through time, as we have record of, God has spoken to man, this involving many and various ways and means. To begin with He spoke directly to Adam and Eve, then came prophets and other ways—to the point that He saw the need for sending His only begotten Son. The Word says, that if we have seen the Son we have seen the Father, because the Son is a perfect mirror of the Father, and He wants to put that mirror in you and me that we will reflect Him at all times through this mirror.

After becoming the sacrifice for our sins, the Son took His rightful place at the right hand side of the throne with

His Father. You see, He brought the new plan to people in person (He being the Master of the plan "of salvation")—through bringing this about He fully experienced death in every single person's place—God is completing the work by making Salvation (Jesus Christ) the suffering that brought victory to each and every one. He (Jesus) freed all from the devil's death hold. He thought of everything, and provided everything that we could ever possibly need. Everything being summed up in Him (Jesus)—everything in heaven and everything on earth—He is so very complete in what He does. It is in Jesus that we find out who we are and, yes, what we are living for. This is not a temporary thing but it is eternal, lasting forever. Praise God!!! He is in charge of it all, having the final word on everything. His plan is so very complete—it is signed, sealed, and delivered, to each and every person.

So, my friends, take a very good look at **Jesus**—He is our all in all, there is none other—He is the center, the beginning, and the end of all we believe, all we look for in the Father God—He is our faith, love, peace, joy, comfort, health, strength, wealth, friend, just to begin naming a few things. <u>Do you love Him more than anything or anybody</u>??????

Please watch your step and do not receive and accept anything that comes from the enemy to cause you to fall. Christ is the one Who has set us free—free to live a life of freedom in Him. The enemy's mission and desire is to steal, kill and destroy, but Jesus gives us victory over him. Your mind can be and will be used by the enemy, but your spirit will not, so listen to your spirit rather than your mind.

God says what He means, and means what He says. His Word is sharper than any two edge sword cutting to the deepest areas of life, cutting through any and every thing, laying us open, and leaving us to listen to and hear Him speak, and obey what we hear. No one is out from under the effect of God's Word—we cannot get away from it, no matter how hard we try—He is everywhere all the time, not missing a single thought or happening.

When the promises that God gives us is undergirded with our faith in Him, then we know that He will do it. All His promises are "yes", so get into them and enjoy the realm of the heavenly Father, that is ours to enjoy. Jesus is our personal High Priest—we do not have a priest that is out of touch with our realities—He represents us to our Father God, and gives us all things. In other words, let us walk right up to Him and get what He is so ready to give us—take all He has to give, He loves giving it all to you— okay?!?!?!?!?!?! God gave His promises to us with His guarantee backed up by His Word—the Word that cannot be broken, and because His Word cannot be broken, then neither can His promises be broken or changeable. Jesus brings us right into the presence of God the Father, under the new covenant—one that really works and puts us in place with the Father, that He has prepared for us. You can go right into the throne room and talk with God the Father.

We are making decisions each and every day and these choices determine the quality of our lives. Be very careful not to live by your own religious plans which could cut you off from Christ. This brings about the need to seek God's guidance for our lives in order to experience His best. Just what is God's best and how do we discover and obtain it? We must first realize that God's ways are the very best, and then we must learn to hear and listen to His voice.

We like to think we can figure out things on our own, so therefore it could be very difficult for many of us to realize that God's way is so much better than ours. We struggle and toil with burdens, and decisions, with the attitude that we do not need help from anyone (even to the place of operating in pride). Surely there is no one who knows our needs better than God does, so we must understand that He longs and desires to help and bless us—not only recognizing this, but running to Him with open arms and spirit, giving Him every jot and tittle of our problems. Rather we see so many living in a degenerate style of life, selfishly grabbing for the supernatural, to be used for their personal gain and satisfaction— this we see going on in many churches.

Allowing understanding of these things and accepting them will cause our spirit to be fertile ground to receive His guidance and instruction. We become His womb for the birthing of what He wants and desires (which surely includes complete obedience in our walk with Him). We welcome the promptings of the Holy Spirit, showing practical insight for our daily lives as we lose ourselves in Him and His Word.

A governing factor of receiving and hearing God's voice will be the peace that He so freely instills in us. This peace is not of the world but it is a peace that He gives which passes all understanding. You see, He also shows and tells you what choices are correct, when you walk in obedience to Him. Do you begin to see how things are starting to open up to you, even though the trials and testings will still come—you have opened up to the Lord to take over and show His power in and through you? He is far greater than any problem that will come against you—you will become more and more consumed in Him, and under His power.

So keep in mind, in all your decision making, that God's best (ways) will far exceed the best that you can ever come up with or even create. God's ways will store you in eternal security as you continue to walk with Him.

Please, stay and walk in fellowship with Him, letting Him birth (we are experiencing and seeing the creation pregnant in many and various ways which will bring birth pangs because the Spirit of God is within us, stirring and wooing every fiber in us so that He can be seen) through these vessels (us) all the things He desires to put into reality. These vessels (us) are His choice to do and show Himself through—we are the channels He chose to use to show Himself in His reality on earth—it was His choice not ours. It is our choice to be free, open, and obedient to Him, so that He can do what He wants and has planned to manifest in and through us.

* * *

God Omnipotent

"As I live and breath, God says,
Every knee will bow before me;
Every tongue will tell the honest truth,
That I and only I am God."
"Those who were never told of Him,
They will see Him!
Those who have never heard of Him,
They will get the message!"
"Are you listening to this? Really listening?!!"
(The Message—Rom 14:11; 15:21)

In this life we must weave carefully, we must spin prayer-fully, we must tend to our knitting because we have our hands full just taking care of our own life before God. Spend time keeping your own walk in life up to par with Him and leave others businesses (alone) and with them. You will have a full time job just keeping yourself laid out before Him. He wants you to be a possessor (one who knows Him) with Him—enjoying your every day and your all the time walk with Him.

**Again, let us say, if we were included in the sin con-
quering death of Jesus, then we are included in the life
conquering resurrection (salvation) that He so freely
gives every one that will accept.**

Jesus Who knew no sin took our sin and put it on
Himself so we could be made right with God. The old life is
gone, the new life is abounding in our lives today that He
might be seen through it all. We are under the power of His
blood—if the blood of animals put on the doors of the
houses in Egypt kept the death angel from coming in, then
think how much more power the blood of Jesus Christ, that
He shed for us, is for us today. It is unlimited, to say the
least—if any limitations are in operation it is because we are
causing them. My Father says that we are to call all things
into being through Him. He is ready and waiting for us to
ask Him for all things.

Hosea said:
"I will call nobodies and make them somebodies;
I will call the unloved and make them beloved.
In the place where they yelled out, "You are nobody!"
They are calling you 'God's living children.'"

Isaiah gave us:
"If each grain of sand on the seashore were numbered
And the sum labeled 'chosen of God,'
They would be numbers still, not names;
Salvation comes by personal selection.
God does not count us; He calls us by name.
Arithmetic is not His focus."
(The Message—Rom 9:25-28)

Do you think you can understand God, His ways, and
His thoughts—can you explain Him? I would readily say to

you, "do not try", just accept Him and His ways, and be what He wants and desires you to be;

> "Everything comes from Him!
> Everything happens through Him;
> Everything ends up in Him.
> Always glory! Always praise!
> Yes++Yes++Yes!!!
> (The Message—Rom 11:36)

The very best thing to do is to take every bit of your life, that includes the great parts and the small parts, that includes all (the whole) of your life, not leaving any thing unhandled, and just throw it all down at His feet—just relinquishing every jot and tittle to Him to take care of. Do not hold back any thing because He knows every thing about you, and the sooner you give it all to Him, the sooner He can and will show Himself through you. Now you can begin to understand yourself by what God is to you, and what He is doing with you—not through and by what you are and what you are doing for Him. You can be one who loves from the heart of God—again, you do not have to understand this, just receive all that He has to give and enjoy His very presence. Please let me say at this time that you will experience a life far greater than anything you could have imagined otherwise.

PRAISE HIM, GIVING HIM GLORY THAT IS DUE HIM!! GLORY FOR NOW AND EVERMORE!! HALLELUJAH!!!!!!!!!!!!

Come, let us shout praises to God Almighty, the Rock Who saved us—If God had not been there, I never would have made it. God is the best, He sculptured the earth by speaking every thing into being—He is great and worth all thousands and thousands of Hallelujahs. If you will not praise Him the very rocks will cry out—the God of glory will last forever, so set your plans to be with Him, forever!

* * *

Bits of Psalms

I want to drink, God,
Deep draughts of God,
I am thirsty for God-alive.
God is a safe place to hide,
Ready to help when we need Him.
Oh, look! God is right here helping!
God is on my side.
Take a good look at Gods' wonders,
They will take your breath away.
Blessed be the Lord,
Day after day He carries us along.
He is our Savior, our God, oh yes!
He is God-for-us, He is God-who-saves-us.
Yours are famous and righteous
Ways, O God.
God, you have done it all!
Who is quiet like you?
You, who made me stare trouble in the face,
Turned me around;
Now let me look life in the face.
I have been to the bottom;

Bring me up, streaming with honors;
Turn to me, be tender to me,
Holy One of Israel.
When I open up in song to you,
I let out lungs full of praise,
My rescued life a song.
All day long I am chanting
About You and Your righteous ways.
What a beautiful home, God of the Angel Armies!
I have always longed to live in a place like this,
Always dreamed of a room in Your house,
Where I could sing for joy to God-alive!
Your love, God, is my song, and I will sing it!
I am forever telling everyone how faithful You are.
I will never quit telling the story of Your love".
"God's Spirit is on and in me;
He has chosen me to preach the message of good
news to the poor, sent me to announce
pardon to prisoners and recovery of sight to the blind,
To set the burdened and battered free,
To announce, 'This is God's time to act!'
The blind see, the lame walk, lepers are cleansed,
the deaf hear, the dead are raised,
The wretched of the earth,
Have God's salvation hospitality extended to them."
"Ask and you will get; seek and you will find;
Knock and the door will open."
"Outsiders and insiders, rejoice together!
People of all nations, celebrate God!
All colors and races, give hearty praise!
Those who were never told of Him,
They will see Him!
Those who have never heard of him,
They will get the message!!!
No one has ever seen or heard anything like this,

Never so much as imagined anything quite like it,
What God has arranged for those who love Him!
(The Message—many varied portions of Psalms).

Don't you understand by now that your body is a sacred place, a place that the Holy Spirit comes and lives in and through? So because of this you cannot live the way you please, ridiculing and squandering what God bought and paid such a price for. You have got to know that God owns it all, the whole works, everything, and wants to show Himself in and through you, <u>His vessel</u>. This makes it so very, very important that we give of our whole self in obedience to God's call and commands.

We sometimes think we know and have all the answers to the questions of this life only to find out or come to the realization that we will never know enough until we fully recognize that God alone has the answers and knows it all. Then we find out that knowing is not everything—some people come to the place of being a know-it-all and treat other people as if they know nothing. We are stressing the importance of not trying to figure God or His ways out but just receive them—relax in His peace and enjoy the fullness of the life He gives you—doing this gives you such peace and feeling of security. We are not to do things for the Lord with the attitude of just receiving things for ourselves—but we are to do and move in and with Him because we are compelled to do it. Jesus Christ gave of Himself for us so the least and the most that we can do, in return and appreciation, is to give Him our all, that He can move through us whenever, wherever, and however He so desires and needs to.

We are not to rank ourselves—we are servants of the Most High, surely not His masters, we are to carry out His every bidding, not to tell Him what and how something is to be done—we are the clay, He is our Potter, He shapes and makes us into different forms and fashions, to fill the situations and get the jobs done, as all members of the same body consisting of many and various parts. We cannot all be the head or the foot or the hand, but we are all what He makes us, working toward the performance of perfection in Him.

My Father is saying, at this time, that He wants me to list some more portions or quotations from the book of Psalms, which are quite timely and fitting:

BITS OF PSALMS

"Train me, God, to walk straight;
Then I will follow your true path.
Put me together, one heart and mind;
Then, undivided, I will worship in joyful fear.
From the bottom of my heart I thank you, dear Lord.
Your love, God, is my song, and I will sing it!
I am forever telling everyone how faithful You are.
I will never quit telling the story of Your love.
'If you will hold on to Me for dear life,' says God,
I will get you out of any trouble.
I will give you the best of care
if you will only get to know and trust Me.
Call Me and I will answer, be at your side in bad times;
I will rescue you, then throw you a party.
I will give you a long life,
Give you a long drink of salvation!
He forgives your sins—every one.
He heals your diseases—every one.
He redeems you from hell—saves your life!
He crowns you with love and mercy—a paradise crown.
He wraps you in goodness—beauty eternal.
He renews your youth—you're always young in His presence.
Thank God! Pray to Him by name!

Tell everyone you meet what He has done!
Oh, thank God—He is so good!
His love never runs out.
Because You have satisfied me, God, I promise
to do everything You say.
What You say goes, God, and stays,
as permanent as the heavens.
Your truth never goes out of fashion;
It is as up-to-date as the earth when the sun comes up.
Your Word and truth are dependable as ever.
Your words are so choice, so tasty;
I prefer them to the best home cooking.
With Your instructions, I understand life.
By Your words I can see where I am going;
They throw a beam of light on my dark path.
I am only concerned with Your plans for me.
Every word You give me is a miracle word,
How could I help but obey?
All you who fear God, how blessed you are!
How happily you walk on His smooth straight road!
Come, bless God, all you servants of God!
Praise the name of God, praise the works of God.
Thank you! Everything in me says 'Thank You!'
Angels listen as I sing my thanks.
I kneel in worship facing Your holy temple
And say it again: 'Thank You!'
Thank You for Your love,
Thank You for Your faithfulness;
Most holy is Your name,
Most holy is Your word.
The moment I called out, you stepped in;
You made my life large with strength.
God, investigate my life;
Get all the facts firsthand.
I am an open book to You;

Even from a distance, You know what I am thinking.
You know when I leave and when I get back;
I am never out of Your sight.
You know everything I am going to say
Before I start the first sentence.
I look behind me and You are there,
Then up ahead and You are there, too,
Your reassuring presence, coming and going.
Your thoughts—how rare, how beautiful!
God, I will never comprehend them!
I could not even begin to count them,
Anymore than I could count the sand of the sea.
Oh, let me rise in the morning and live always with
You!
Investigate my life, God,
Get a clear picture of what I am about;
See for Yourself whether I have done anything wrong,
Then guide me on the road to eternal life.
Post a guard at my mouth, God,
Set a watch at the door of my lips.
Don't let me so much as dream of evil
Or thoughtlessly fall into bad company.
God always does what He says,
And is gracious in everything He does.
Praise God in His holy house of worship,
Praise Him under the open skies;
Praise Him for His acts of power,
Praise Him for His Magnificent greatness;
Let every living, breathing creature praise God!"
(The Message—many varied versus from Psalms)
HALLELUJAH!!!!HALLELUJAH!!!!
HALLELUJAH!!!

* * *

Could I now bring it to your attention, that God is present with you, walking right by your side to keep you on track and from falling (He even orders His angels to keep watch over you to keep you from stumbling). You have everything, you just have to appropriate and use it—you have got it all—all God's gifts are right there with you or in front of you. You do not have to run all over the world looking for something because it is right there with you, all you have to do is align yourself with the Father and receive the manifestation of His power and glory—realize and know that He loves you this much, He will never turn His back on you!! He glories in your acceptance and willingness to Him—you have been set apart to walk a God-filled, God-loved, and God-powered life with Him, because it is Him living through and with us, none of ourselves, all Him. He knows what He is doing and He fills us to overflowing with His thoughts and ways—we do not have to understand, just be available and obedient, open and willing, He will take over and show His capabilities through us. I love Him and His ways, don't you?

The powers of darkness are cruel, devastating, and so very destructive, they foul up the life of man in so many and various, devilish, evil ways—that is just what they were meant to be—the enemy or thief has one mission, that is to steal and kill and destroy, but our Jesus came that we might have real life and that eternal, far more and better life than we ever dreamed of or could dream of.

Now, let me continue to be obedient to my Father, He is saying He wants me to list the following; I sense in my spirit that He knows that someone needs it, so here goes;

Ps 102:25-27 *In the beginning You laid the foundations of the earth, and the heavens are the work of Your hands. They will perish, but You remain; they will all wear out like a garment. Like clothing You will change them and they will be discarded. But You remain the same, and Your years will never end.*

Problems and heartaches come and can overwhelm us and cause us to feel just like God has rejected us; but He Who is our Creator is eternally with us and surely will keep all His promises; yes, even though we feel so alone. The world will perish, but God our "Father" will remain.

Heb 1:10-12...*In the beginning, O Lord, You laid the foundations of the earth, and the heavens are the work of Your hands. They will perish, but You remain; they will all wear out like a garment. You will roll them up like a robe; like a garment they will be changed. But You remain the same, and Your years will never end.*

In Psalms the writer regards God as the speaker and applies the words to His Son Jesus. Jesus' authority is established over all of creation—so we dare not treat any created object or earthly resource as more important than He is. The Jews accepted the Old Testament, but most of them rejected Jesus as the coming Messiah. The recipients of the Hebrew letter seem to have been Jewish Christians who were experiencing rejection of their fellow Jews, to the place of often feeling isolated and wanting to exchange the life with Christ for their old faith. ***Boldly,*** **very boldly,** I say, **Christ is our only security** in a changing world like we live in. Whatever happens to this world, our Christ will remain changeless. If we continue to trust Him we will be eternally and absolutely secure. ***On Christ the solid Rock I stand, all other ground is sinking sand.*** Christ's character will never change; He persistently shows His love to us, He is always just, fair, and merciful to all who are so undeserving, but yet will reach out to Him for help—so be very thankful that He is changeless and will always be there to help you when you need Him and give you forgiveness when you sin and fall. Col 1:16 *For by Him all things were created; things in heaven and on earth, visible and invisible, whether thrones or powers or* *rulers or authorities; all things were created by Him and for Him.*

Christ has no equal and no rival, He is Lord of all, His creation including the spiritual world and the government. Everything got started in Him and finds its purpose in Him, absolutely everything, above and below, and yes, visible and invisible—He is God's original purpose in all creation. Every time we think of Jesus let us thank God for His Son, Who He gave for us. Now do you want to be His Bride? That is what it is all about, He is collecting and preparing a bride for His Son.

More over, besides giving His Son for us, He goes even farther to show His love to and for us. Heb 1:14 *Are not all angels ministering spirits sent to minister for those who will inherit salvation???* He gives His angels charge over us, as believers, to guard us in our walk with Him, look at Ps 91:11, also Mat 18:10; Lk 16:22; Acts 12:7; etc., and to proclaim His message Rev 14:6-12; and carrying out and executing His judgment Acts 12:1-23; Rev 20:1-3. Be ever attentive to the appearance, the presence, and action of His angels in His watching out and over you. In other words, He is not limited at all in His ways of doing and getting things done, the limitation is us, not Him.

* * *

Your Motivation

Self-motivation is the inner drive
that puts optimism into action.
<u>Winners are driven by desire.</u>
I am motivated everyday by my current thoughts.
Motive is that which is in the individual—
rather than that which is outside—
which moves us into action.
Winners in life have developed ability to move
toward their goals in action.
Desire is a strong positive magnet that pulls to
achieve goals with memories of pleasure and success—
emotional estate of where you are and where you
want to be thus striving toward goals.
Don't dwell on a reverse idea.
Desire sparks activity, coming from within—
success depends on drive—
persistence, out of need, brings desire.
Replace fear motivation with desire motivation.
Concentrate on solution rather than the problem.
Make desire your current motivating thought.
Positive self-expectancy includes;

enthusiasm, optimism, and winning.
Self-expectancy is number one step toward winning.
You become that which you fear—
what do you expect for yourself?
Remember you receive what you expect—
expect nothing less than the best.
Look at problems as opportunities.
Learn to stay relaxed and friendly.
Instead of griping, try praising,
Instead of cynicism, try optimism,
Instead of being critical, try being helpful,
Get excited and enthusiastic about your dreams.
Excitement is like a forest fire, you can smell it,
taste it, and see it a mile away.
Positive self-expectancy is the attitude of inner faith that
generates the inner drive to action which is
self-motivation.

* * *

Be extremely careful and aware of the working of the mind for out of it comes the sins of violence or vileness— these originate in your mind. The thoughts that you think in this life molds your character—if you think evil then you will act evil, if you think righteous and holy then you will be righteous and holy—your outward man is controlled by the inner man. I find the spirit of anti-christ is working among people in such subtle and deceiving ways, that people are not aware of his presence, but anything that can or does work at controlling your thoughts in contrariwise ways that are not completely on Jesus—watch out. We have to take the weapons of warfare that the Lord clothes us with (all the armor, every piece that the Lord gives us) and pull down and destroy the strongholds that have been built up against us— rendering them helpless, powerless, and removing them from the presence of the vessel of the Lord.

Mk 7:21-23....*For from within, out of the heart of men, proceed evil thoughts, adulteries, fornications, murders, thefts, covetousness, wickedness, deceit, lasciviousness, an evil eye, blasphemy, pride, foolishness; all these things come from within, and defile the man.*

We must keep our minds stayed and dependant upon and in Christ, under the power of God, and full of the Holy Spirit—this is the only way that we can reflect the fullness of God's beauty while showing forth His love. Let His grace and the evidence of His power be manifested in and through our lives at all times.

In giving our minds to Him, we become aware of our every thought, desire, and choice being fashioned in and on His thoughts—you see, you are beginning to give your spirit control over your mind now. This will produce holy living in our bodies just as it does in the soul. As we think beautiful thoughts, it begins to leave impressions in our nature and, yes, in our very fleshly bodies. It is this power of God that dissolves diseases, and also restores diseased tissues that may be attached to the body. It is satan that sends and applies the unclean and impure symptoms of disease upon our fleshly bodies—it is Jesus that heals and takes away the same. The Holy Spirit flows through and lives in this temple or our body, and as He is given full opening in His temple then He likes to clean it and keep it clean.

1 Thess 5:23-24....*I pray God your whole spirit and soul and body be preserved blameless unto the coming of our Lord Jesus Christ. Faithful is He that calls you Who also will do it.*

Let the Holy Spirit, through your spirit, control your every thought, every step, every move—then the precious blood of Jesus Christ will flow through you showing Himself in sufficient ways to get everything done that He wants done.

There is and never will be any unholy comment that comes from the lips of Jesus that would jar or cause the spirit of another to slip or fall. When He controls our mind and thoughts we will not say anything to deter or cause another to slip. When our minds have been sanctified through the Holy Spirit, people will know it, they will feel it, they will know it is not our minds but the mind of the Lord.

Dear ones, forget about understanding or even trying to understand the Lord, forget about your self-confidence, it is no good, just rally (get lost) in God-confidence. It does not matter what comes your way, heart-aches, temptations, trials of any kind, they have already been sent to others before you, that had to face them—you are not the first to be confronted by them, but our God is sufficient, He is our all, He is the One that fights our battles, so we already know that we are victorious in and through Him. Just remember that God will never let you down, He will see you through any and everything, He will not let you be pushed beyond your limits. GLORY!!!

We have the very life of Christ in us, lifting us up into what He is, rather than us pulling Him down to what we are. What it amounts to is; He wants and has to have us, all of us or nothing, He wants us to live in abundance that He supplies, living a Godly life, showing and leading others to do the same in their lives. He expects us to give Him every thing we have and everything we are, running for the prize of His high calling, and not missing it but winning, because He has given us this kind of relationship. Let's not come up short of what is expected of us.

Rev 22:1...And he showed me a pure river of water of life, clear as crystal, proceeding out of the throne of God and of the Lamb.

As you submit your mind along with everything else to Him, you are fulfilling the desire of God to come into the real life, the life that is being lived with Jesus Christ the

Lord—this is the expectation of the Father God as He says, "The Spirit and the Bride say come"—I am surely included in His Bride, (are you?), please, come and be possessed by Him. So in everything, do it wholeheartedly and freely to God's glory, nothing else mattering.

Let me list something that will give you a good picture of how things could and might be for some:

The night that Jesus came

It was the night that Jesus came, and through the house,
Not a person was praying, not one in the house.
The Bible was left on the shelf, without care,
For no one thought Jesus would come through there.
The children were dressing to crawl into bed,
Not once ever kneeling or bowing their head.
And mom, in the rocking chair, with baby on her lap,
Was watching the late show, as I took a nap.
When out of the east, there rose such a clatter,
I sprang to my feet to see what is the matter.
Away to the window I flew like a flash,
Tore open the shutters and lifted the sash.
When what to my wandering eyes should appear,
But angels proclaiming that Jesus was here.
The light of His face made me cover my head,
It was Jesus returning, just as He had said.
And though I possessed worldly wisdom and wealth,
I cried when I saw Him, in spite of myself.
In the Book of Life, which He held in His hand,
Was written the name of every saved man.
He spoke not a word, as He search for my name,
then He said, "It is not here", I hung my head in shame.
The people whose name's had been written with love,
He gathered to take to His Father above.

With those who were ready, He rose without a sound,
While all the others were left, standing around.
I fell to my knees, but it was too late,
I had waited too long, and thus sealed my fate.
I stood and I cried as those rose out of sight,
oh, if only I had known that this was the night.
In the words of this poem, the meaning is clear,
The coming of Jesus is drawing very near.
There is only one life, and when comes the call,
We will all find out, that the Bible was true after all.

* * *

I love the way *(The Message)* defines LOVE;
1Cor 13
Love never gives up.
Love cares more for others than for self.
Love does not want what it does not have.
Love does not strut.
Love does not have a swelled head.
Love does not force itself on others.
Love is not always "me first",
Love does not fly off the handle,
Love does not keep score of sins of others,
Love does not revel when others grovel,
Love takes pleasure in the flowering of truth,
Love puts up with anything,
Love trusts God always,
Love always looks for the best,
Love never looks back,
Love keeps going to the end.

* * *

Never again let anyone talk you into or lead you into getting back in the path of the ways of the world because Christ
has set you free from this, that you might walk and talk and
live a truly free life. Now we are to think of ourselves as the
way that He thought of Himself. He was not pushy, He was
constantly looking for someway to help others, so we are to
forget ourselves long enough to help others when they need
help, if someone falls into sin, forgivingly help restore them,
share their burdens, fulfilling the law of Christ. These are
some ways to celebrate God, showing everyone that you
meet that Christ is love and He is loving all. God wants to
clothe you with strength, humility, kindness, compassion, to
name a few—but regardless of what you put on, you are to
wear **love** as your base garment, never being without it—
then no matter what happens, you can be cheerful and thankful to and for your God. Exercise and cultivate your walk
with Him daily so that people will see your maturity in Him,
and receive Him as their personal Savior.

Jesus said that "narrow is the way and few there be that
find and enter it"—this narrow way is from faith to faith seeing Jesus as our Just One, our Holy One, listening to His
voice. The narrow way is from faith to faith until we become
the just who live by faith, this faith being engulfed and controlled by His love. All this is included in our progress of
faith to faith by sitting at the feet of Jesus and learning from
Him—we have no other means or source that offers and
gives us this type of eternal life. Again, it is your choice, you
choose how and where you will spend eternity, what is your
choice? After reading this, can you see or find any other
choice but the Lord Jesus Christ, I really and truly think not,
because I have been where some of you might be, and now
I am where I am in Him—dear ones, there is no comparison,
just love, joy, peace, comfort, power, with Him constantly
and continually showering His blessings on me. It is difficult
to find the words to try to begin to express the reality of this

life with Him, believe me, you just have to experience it to
know—come away, dearly beloved, come away with Him,
He is the One, the only One, the Just One, the Glorious One,
the Holy One, the Sanctifier, Who loves you so very dearly.

* * *

You will find listed below some very interesting and
helpful questions that the Lord sent my way:

1. Why should I continue to condemn myself when
   God has forgiven me of my sins?
2. Is my self-condemnation drawing me closer to God?
3. What good am I doing to continually condemn
   myself?
4. Is this helping my relationship to others?
5. Is my self-condemnation influencing God?
6. Is there any scriptural basis for condemning myself?
7. How long will I continue to condemn myself?

How to forgive myself:
1. An honest confession of specific wrongs.
2. Reaffirm my faith in God's promises.
3. Release myself by an act of my will.

* * *

As I am sitting here writing all these things and thinking
on them, it comes to me that I can and should do the same
thing that Paul has done, so here goes;

I ask the God of our Master, Jesus Christ, the God of
glory to make us intelligent and discerning in knowing Him
personally, our eyes focused and clear, so that we can see
exactly what it is He is calling us to do, grasp the immensity
of this glorious way of life He has for Christians—oh, the

utter extravagance of His work in us who trust Him—endless, boundless strength!!! All this strength issues from Christ—God raised Him from death and set Him on a throne in deep heaven, in charge of running the universe, everything from galaxies to governments, no name and no power exempt from His rule. And not just for the time being, but *forever and eternity.* He is in charge of it all, has the final word on everything. At the center of all this, Christ rules the church. The church, you see, is not peripheral (the church is in this world but spiritually is not of this world) to the world; the world is peripheral to the church. The church (His church) is Christ's body, in which He speaks and acts, by which He fills everything with His presence.

My response is to get down on my knees before the Father God, this magnificent Father Who parcels out all heaven and earth. I ask Him to strengthen us by His Spirit—not a brute strength but a glorious inner strength—that Christ will live in us as we open the door and invite Him in. And I ask Him that with both feet planted firmly in love, we will be able to take in, with all Christians, the extravagant dimensions of Christ's love. Reach out and experience the width of His love! Test its length of His love! Plumb the depths of His love! Rise to the heights of His love! Live full lives in His love, full in the fullness of God Almighty.

* * *

He Is an Awesome Father God

Glory to God in the church!
Glory to God in the Messiah, in Jesus!
Glory down all the generations!
Glory through all millennia! Oh, yes!
"He climbed the high mountain,
He captured the enemy and seized the booty,
He handed it all out in gifts to us His people."
(The Message—Eph 3:21; 4:8)

God looks after us all,
Makes us robust with life.
Blessed are you who give yourselves over to God,
Turn your backs on the world's "sure thing".
What is more, our hearts brim with joy,
Since we have taken for our own His holy name!
God, my God,
I cannot thank You enough!!!!
(The Message)

* * *

Let me say at this time that the things I have said and
listed on the pages of this book are directed by my Father

God through His Spirit—my purpose and desire is wanting to stress and bring forth the very intimate feelings that I have experienced and am experiencing at the present time; these are not feelings that I have dreamed up but very real and very available to each and everyone. I teach and express or relate to you only the things that He tells me to do. The Spirit brings and makes life (He is the Bread of Life that came down from heaven)—sheer muscle and will-power (the flesh) does not make anything happen. Every word that I have spoken to you are Spirit-words and came through the Spirit, bringing and giving life. Again, you are making choices, either to accept, receive, and bring into action the Spirit of Father God in your life, or you are choosing to go or continue to go the way of the flesh. It is just that simple, the choice is ours, He does not force anyone, but He honors each and every choice we make. Please, remember, that Jesus said "I am the Bread of Life, whoever believes in Me has real life, eternal life—as you eat of this Bread of Life you will live with Me eternally, forever!" What Jesus taught was from the One Who sent Him, so when you hear the teaching of Jesus you are hearing the teaching from Father God the Most High One. When you follow Him, the Light of the world, the Prophet of God, you will not stumble around in the darkness. The world does not know the first thing about victorious living, so how can it lead you into this kind of life? It can't—Jesus poured out His blood through His experience on the cross so that we can be free—*abundantly free*. It is in Jesus that we find out who we are and what we are living for. Through Him we share the same Holy Spirit and have open access to the same Father God. Father God is building His building, putting us all into it, as brick by brick, with Jesus as the Cornerstone holding it all together—it is taking shape continually, day after day, a temple in which God can feel at home with and in. Even though we are members of the same body, that does not mean that we are to look, speak or act exactly the same, because He has given each of us varying and different gifts and talents to be used to get His job done. By the way, He expects us to keep company with Him and learn the fullness of His love to us—He says He wants us to be courteously reverent to one another through His love.

Please understand a reality of the cross—since the cross, will you not know, that satan is a **defeated foe**!!! Yes, satan was defeated—he thought he was being victorious by causing Jesus to be put on the cross but not so, he was the one that was being defeated. Now we have the authority and power to control him rather than him controlling us.

* * *

Let me list a few characteristics of some of the Old Testament personnel:

Faith of Abraham
Meekness of Moses
Courage of Joshua
Concern of Nehemiah
Tears of Jeremiah
Praises of David

This is just a beginning of listing a few of the men of God that He used in fulfilling His plan to bring it to where we are at the present, but it does give you an idea of the walk of life involved in each and every situation—all these happening before Jesus came and went to the cross. So how much more should we give of ourselves to Him in this present time—He is our all in all!!! GLORY!! GLORY!

* * *

So leave the corruption and compromise;
Leave it for good, says God.
Don't link up with those who will pollute you.

I want you all for Myself.
I will be a Father to you;
You will be sons and daughters to me.
The Word of the Master, God.
(The Message—11 Cor 6:16-18)

* * *

God has not promised
Skies always blue,
Flower strewn pathways
All our lives through;
God has not promised
Sun without rain,
Joy without sorrow,
Peace without pain.
But God has promised
Strength for the day,
Rest from our labor,
Light for our way,
Grace for all our trials,
His help from above,
His unfailing sympathy,
And His undying love.
Yes, God shall wipe away all tears
Never to return to our eyes,
When He takes us home to be with Him.
Ever since You took my hand, Lord,
I am on the right way.
Since You have got my feet on the life path,
I am all radiant from the shining of Your face.
I have a good thing going and I am not letting go.
(Author Unknown)

* * *

In Closing

And that about wraps it up—God is so strong, and He wants you strong; so take everything He has set before you, well made weapons of the best materials—and put them to use that you will be able to stand up to everything the devil throws at you or your way. Very true, this is no afternoon athletic contest that we will walk away from and forget in a couple of hours, that it ever happened. This is for real, for keeps, a life-or-death fight to the finish against the devil and all his demons. You are up against far more than you can handle on your own, so be prepared, take every weapon that God has given and issued to you and use these weapons victoriously, so that when the battle is over you will be standing on your feet, shouting the song of victory to God Almighty. *(Finally, be strong in the Lord and in His mighty power. Put on the full armor of God so that you can take your stand against the devil's schemes. For our struggle is not against flesh and blood, but against the rulers, against the authorities, against the powers of this dark world and against the spiritual forces of evil in the heavenly*

realms. Therefore put on the full armor of God, so that when the day of evil comes, you may be able to stand your ground, and after you have done everything, to stand. Stand firm then, with the belt of truth buckled around your waist, with the breastplate of righteousness in place, and with your feet fitted with the readiness that comes from the gospel of peace. In addition to all this, take up the shield of faith, with which you can extinguish all the flaming arrows of the evil one. Take the helmet of salvation and the sword of the Spirit, which is the word of God. And pray in the Spirit on all occasions with all kinds of prayers and requests. With this in mind, be alert and always keep praying for all the saints— Eph 6:10-18—KJV)

Do you see the time for celebration? You can celebrate because you know how it is going to turn out—everything that God wants to do in and through you and me will be done, if we yield to Him. I do not expect to be embarrassed in the very least because I am His—this life versus even more life, I cannot lose. Just think of it, there is a celebration in heaven every time a lost one comes and accepts the Lord as their personal Saviour.

The Lost Sheep

Once upon a time a little lamb was lost,
The good shepherd went seeking, no matter what the cost!
Ninety-nine? No, that will never do,
I must seek and search until I find you!
Come to Me My loved one, come!
I have redeemed you through the blood of My Son.
Just think of the celebration when you are found,
And loosed from the kingdom of darkness, where you
have been bound.
Many more are wondering, gone astray,
No good shepherd to lead them, day by day!
Will you be the one My message to take?
Hurry!!!! Hurry!!!! Their souls are at stake!
Go into all the world I command you,
Preach My gospel, they need to know me too!
Here is My desire for all,
For those who will answer the call.

Psalm 23
Walking by the shepherd's side
that's where we will always abide.
What more could we need,
on green pastures we feed,
He leads us beside the still waters to rest,
Oh, how greatly our souls are blessed!
From the living waters we drink,
We wade in deep, He will never let us sink!
It is written we will never thirst no more,
If we drink from His abundant store,
Rivers in the desert we will see,
rivers of life flowing free,
To a lost and hurting world,
the blood banner is unfurled.

Isaiah 61:1-3
Beauty instead of ashes,
The oil of joy instead of mourning,
The garment of praise instead of a failing spirit,
We are called oaks of righteousness,
The planting of the Lord that He may be glorified!

Isaiah 61:10-11
We are covered by the robe of righteousness,
As a bridegroom decks himself with a garland,
And as a bride adorns herself with her jewels,
As surely as the earth brings forth its' shoots,
As a garden causes what is sown in it to grow,
So surely the Lord God will cause righteousness,
justice, and praise to spring forth before all the nations
through the self propelling power of His Word.
In righteous paths He leads us, for His names' sake,
Desiring that we lead others this eternal way to take.
We shall have no fear,

In the valley of the shadow of death, the shepherd is here,
His rod to correct, His staff to guide,
They are a comfort as onward we stride.
He has prepared the table before us,
Out of the way the enemy He thrusts,
His blessings so abundant and free,
Brimming cups running over for you and me.
He anoints our heads with oil,
Through the Holy Spirits' power we toil.

Psalm 18:33
Upon the high places with hinds feet we leap,
Able to make progress, the enemies to defeat!

Psalm 57:9-11
We will praise and give thanks to you, O Lord,
Among the peoples and the nations sing praises,
Your mercy and loving kindness are great,
Reaching to the heavens,
Your truth and faithfulness to the clouds,
Be exalted, Oh God, above the heavens,
Let Your glory be over all the earth,
goodness, mercy, and unfailing love,
Are blessings sent down from above.
They will follow us all the days of our life.
As we walk together husband and wife.
One day the trump of God we will hear,
Oh how short the time, it is so near,
Our precious Savior will appear,
To catch away His bride to be by His side
forever in the house of the Lord to abide!
(©Beverly Gould 7-23-02)

* * *

The Wedding Bells

Ring, Ring, those wedding bells,
Ring them out throughout the land,
There is going to be a wedding,
There is going to be a wedding,
And the bride is ready for the groom.

What a day that's going to be,
When He comes back for you and me,
There is going to be a wedding,
There is going to be a wedding,
For the bride is ready for the groom.

* * *

I thank you each and everyone for spending quality time in the pages of this book. It is my prayer that you have seen Father God and have made the choice to walk with Him all the days of your life.

This is a sure thing:
If we die with Him, we will live with Him;
If we stick it out with Him, we will rule with Him;
If we turn our backs on Him, he'll turn His back on us;
If we give up on Him, He does not give up—
for there is no way He can be false to Himself.
(The Message—11 Tim 2:11-13)

When you believe in God it alters your language.
Accepting the love of God affects your relationships.
When you accept the hope of God it enters into your work.
We cannot get too much of God.
We cannot get too much faith and obedience.
We cannot get too much love and worship of God.

When we receive Wisdom we have skill in living,
Now you have a brand new life in Jesus Christ,
With and worth everything to live for.
When we worship God it will almost certainly
bring the depths of joy and urgency.

The way of the Cross Leads Home

(The song)
I must need go home by the way of the cross,
There is no other way but this;
I shall never get sight of the Gates of Light,
If the way of the cross I miss.
I must need go on in the blood sprinkled way,
The path that my Savior trod,
If I ever climb to the heights sublime,
Where the soul is at home with God.
Then I bid farewell to the way of the world,
To walk in it nevermore;
For my Lord says "Come", and I seek my home,
Where He waits at the open door.

Sitting at the Feet of Jesus

(the song)
Sitting at the feet of Jesus, O what words I hear Him say!
Happy place, so near, so precious!
May it find me there each day!
Sitting at the feet of Jesus, I would look upon the past!
For His love has been so gracious,
It has won my heart at last.
Sitting at the feet of Jesus, where can mortal be more blest,
There I lay my sins and sorrows,
and when weary, find sweet rest.

Sitting at the feet of Jesus, there I love to weep and pray,
While I from His fullness gather
grace and comfort ev'ry day.
Bless me, O my Savior bless me, as I sit low at Thy feet!
O look down in love upon me,
let me see Thy face so sweet!
Give me, Lord the mind of Jesus, make me holy as He is;
May I prove I've been with Jesus,
who is all my righteousness.
Sitting at the feet of Jesus, watching, waiting everyday,
Trusting in His grace and power,
safe to keep me all the way.
List'ning at the feet of Jesus, His command to go or stay,
Trusting always in His wisdom, safe to guide when I obey.
Seeking still the feet of Jesus, I would seek no other place,
For 'tis there I claim the promise,
of the fullness of His grace.
When the toils of life are over,
when my race on earth is run;
May the evening shadows gathering,
find me there when day is done.
Sitting at the feet of Jesus, where I love to kneel and pray,
Till His goodness and His glory,
drive the shadows from my way.

* * *

May I leave you with the following decision:

I make a lifetime decision of quality
And hereby declare the following in the name of Jesus...
In the presence of the Father and Holy Spirit...
Even before satan and his demons.
The Word of God is the absolute Truth in my life.
I make it the final authority to settle all questions that con-

*front me. I choose to agree with the Word of God
and I choose to disagree with any thoughts, conditions,
or circumstances contrary to His Word.
Jesus is my Lord and Savior, He resides within me,
I know who I am in Christ Jesus; a child of God,
a partaker of His divine nature and His inheritance.
Jesus has given me authority over all the power of the
enemy, so I am master over satan and his forces.
Jesus is my Source, my total supply.
He paid the full price at Calvary by giving His all for my
redemption and for the full provision of all my need.
I put my trust in Him and His faithfulness to His Word that
all the redemption benefits belong to me because I belong
to Him. I depend only on the completed work of Jesus. In
everything I give praise and thanks to the
Lord in simple obedience to His Word. I WILL to love my
fellow beings because I love the Lord. I ask the Father to
give me genuine thankfulness and love as I step out in faith
to be a doer of His Word—depending not on my feelings,
but on His Word.
Since I am born of God, I overcome the world.
I take any problems as an opportunity to be an overcomer,
counting it all joy because God's Word says He always
causes me to triumph in Christ Jesus.
Since God's Holy Spirit dwells in me and Jesus promised
that He will never leave me, I am confident that I can and
will adhere to this "decision of quality" until the Lord
Jesus comes in His Glory and I will go to be with
HIM forever and forever!!!!!!!!!!*

*IN JESUS' NAME
I LOVE YOU JESUS*

IN THE POTTER'S IMAGE

IN THE POTTER'S HANDS WAS HELD A SHAPELESS
LUMP OF CLAY,
NOT A BIT OF BEAUTY AS IN THOSE HANDS IT
LAY.
WHAT DID THE POTTER SEE AS HE LOOKED AT IT
THIS DAY?
IS IT REALLY WORTH HIS TIME, WOULD THE
EFFORT REALLY PAY?

HE PUT IT DOWN UPON THE WHEEL,
AND AROUND AND AROUND IT SPUN;
HE WOULD NOT QUIT THE PROCESS UNTIL HIS
WORK WAS DONE!
HIS EYES WERE FIXED INTENTLY, AS A SHAPE
BEGAN TO FORM,
HE SAW THE POTTER'S IMAGE IN WHAT WAS
BEING BORN.

YOU, MY LORD, ARE THE POTTER, I AM THE CLAY,
THE WORK OF YOUR HANDS IS WHAT THE WORD
HAS TO SAY.
O LORD, TO THE WILL OF THE POTTER I YIELD,
TO EACH STROKE AND FORM YOUR LOVING
HANDS WIELD.

ALL WORKS TOGETHER FOR GOOD WE ARE
TOLD,
FOR THOSE WHO LOVE GOD, HIS DESIGN WILL
UNFOLD.
WITHOUT YOU MY POTTER, I AM WRETCHED,
NAKED, AND BLIND,
THROUGH YOUR FURNACE I GO TO BECOME
GOLD REFINED.

WITH WHITE RAIMENT YOU'LL CLOTH ME ON
THE GLORIOUS DAY,
AS IN YOUR HOLY PRESENCE, I WILL FOREVER
STAY!
BOWING DOWN BEFORE YOU, YOU ARE WORTHY
TO BE PRAISED!
REFLECTING YOUR IMAGE—I AM TOTALLY
AMAZED.

OH, MY FAITHFUL POTTER, UNTIL THAT DAY,
SUBMISSIVE TO YOUR LOVING HANDS I STAY,
LET ME REFLECT YOUR IMAGE THIS VERY DAY,
TO THOSE WHO ARE LOST AND KNOW NOT THE
WAY!
SO ALL YOUR VESSELS BEFORE YOU WILL BOW,
TO THIS I AM COMMITTED—TO THIS I VOW!
(Beverly Gould—8-22-02)

Printed in the United States
1050700003B/274-324